## At Home and Away

by Michael Lund

This five-volume novel series chronicles an American family during times of peace and war from 1915 to 2015. The first book, *Route 66 Sweetheart*, is set mostly in and around Rutherford, New Jersey, during the 1930s. *Route 66 Dreamer* features the son of a Swedish immigrant who pursues his dreams of American success in Kansas and Missouri in the early 1940s. However, in both books some family members move away to distant countries and unexpected challenges.

This third volume, *Route 66 Looking-glass*, takes place primarily in Missouri in the mid-1960s, but characters also travel far from home and familiar experiences. *Farewell, Route 66* (Book Four) will follow another generation of family members, this time from Missouri to Southeast Asia where many learn, sadly, "how to not tell a war story." In the final volume of the series, *Route 66 Redux*, the next generation travels to Europe, Central America, and the Middle East to understand their identity in a multi-national community.

## Acknowledgments

As is frequently claimed in detective stories, we have our usual cast of suspects. In this case, they are guilty only of helping me. And I am grateful.

First, we have the generous publisher, Dr. Bud Banis, whose business acumen keeps BeachHouse Books alive and well in a period of rapid technological and economic change. His love of books is a greater motive than a desire for profit, and he consistently reminds me of what is best in our entrepreneurial culture. There is the knowledgeable editor, Jim Shifflett, whose understanding of history, literature, grammar, and style has informed every page that follows. And John Lund, the genius of graphic design, transformed the shadowy images in my head into striking, memorable forms and colors.

This book is for my parents and their generation, who, looking into the mirror at mid-life, found valuable lessons to pass on to their children. It is my hope that we all follow their example.

# Route 66 Looking-glass

Michael Lund

BeachhouseBooks

Saint Charles Missouri USA

*Route 66 Looking-glass*

# Copyright 2014 Michael Lund

# Cover Design by John Lund

*ISBN9781596300910*

beachhousebooks.com

Publication date 2014

Library of Congress LCCN 2 0 1 4 9 1 4 7 6 4

**BeachHouse Books**

www.beachhousebooks.com

an Imprint of
Science & Humanities Press
63 Summit Pointe Ct
Saint Charles, MO 63301-0571

# Route 66 Looking-glass

## Michael Lund

### 2014

# Prologue: Lenticular Images

"Here's something I found deep in a desk drawer," I said to my son Curtis, pulling a forty-year-old Cracker Jack prize from my pocket. It was a plastic novelty card that shows one image if looked at straight on, but another when tilted.

He smiled, "Ah, the wonderful King Kong/Empire State Building picture! Viewed in one way—" he manipulated the plastic rectangle, "this shows the skyscraper against a clear sky."

"But turned the other way," I noted, "you see King Kong clutching Faye and swatting at fighter planes. It's a two-sided coin with only one face."

"Yes. What do they call these things—'lenticular images,' I think. But what are you doing at age 98 playing with children's toys?"

We were in the family room of his spacious old home in northeastern North Carolina on the Monday following a family celebration of my birthday. "I guess I'm reminiscing about you children becoming adults in the 1960s and leaving such playthings behind. I was going through some old papers, clearing out where I can so you won't have so much to do when—when I pass on to my great reward."

I had downsized when I moved from Missouri nine years ago, giving up my four-bedroom house to live in a retirement apartment. Approaching 100 years of age, I feel I should be reducing my material possessions even more.

"Nana," he protested. "You're going to outlive us all! Plus you've got more volumes of the family saga to compose."

A few years ago I began filling Curtis in on some lesser known aspects of our family history. (For instance, his younger sister had her own double-image toy, a naughty one. When she turned it this way and that repeatedly, the figures moved, creating a very brief, flip-book movie effect that would have amused her brothers — and floored her father.)

"I do have a few more things to do in this life. For now, take a look at this study of X-ray scattering." I handed him a scientific paper from which I had obscured the author's name.

He puzzled over it. "Hmm. Another relic of the past? 'Equilibrium properties of liquids,' 'elastic neutron scattering,' 'a collimated, monochromatic X-ray beam.' I'm supposed to understand this? It looks like something Carol wrote." Carol, the younger sister, was now a mathematician and computer programmer.

"Close. It was authored by your dear father in the mid-1960s. Quite impressive, really."

"You understand it? My goodness, my 97-year-old mother learned more than I thought back then, or she must be going back to school in what—quantum physics?"

I laughed. "I don't have any idea what this is about. But I know that your father was very proud when it was published and it received recognition."

Curtis handed it back. "Well, this English professor shares your lack of understanding. But why are you asking that I demonstrate my ignorance?"

"Because, like the Cracker Jack prize--and a good many other things that come from that time--this represents more than scientific advancement, at least to me."

"I'm ready to learn, especially if you translate into another sphere of knowledge."

"Well, when your father was doing the research for this paper, he was at the peak of his powers as a theoretical physicist. Not that he didn't continue as a research scholar and a great teacher for another fifteen years, but he enjoyed his work more then than at any later time. That was an era when science was genuinely respected, and I was appropriately proud of him."

"A member of the Sputnik generation, I understand. That moving light in the sky--visible to the naked eye--challenged us to beat the Soviets into space and into the future. So the nation poured resources into research and development, and people like Dad were models."

"Oscar had his first Ph.D. students in those years, and he saw in them his own youthful energy, eager to take up new challenges. One of your father's students was even part of the cadre of researchers that took us to the moon."

"His own children helped mostly by getting out of his hair! Let's see, Louis was starting law school, I was an undergraduate English major, and Carol was heading off to the University of Missouri, following Dad in the study of physics--or so we thought."

That period was satisfying in many ways for Oscar and me. Our children were fulfilling the promise they'd always shown, and we were comfortable in our routines. It was a good time for much of the country as well, reaping the benefits of post-war prosperity.

When, earlier today, I had first looked at the double image, I saw it too as a positive statement about America's strength. Here was the tallest building in the world during my childhood and much of my adulthood. (It would, though, be surpassed by the World Trade Center, then returned to primacy after 9/11, at least in terms of buildings in Manhattan.)

Although King Kong was a fictional beast supposedly found on a remote Pacific island, he became an American icon, symbol of our ability to control the savage energy of nature (and what we think of as untamed human nature). We needed that reassurance in 1933, the beginning of the Depression. My husband Oscar knew that well, as his father, a builder and master carpenter, struggled to support his small family in those years.

4

Kong's vulnerability to passive female beauty also fed our ideas about gender in the 1930s: males have physical strength and mechanical ability, while women must protect their fragile beauty in order to control, to a small extent, their destiny. When war came at the end of that decade, people would begin to learn that we needed the physical abilities of Rosie the Riveter and the intellectual power of—well, female medical technologists like me.

Looking back to the 60s, though, I also see storm clouds on the national horizon, and not just the Civil Rights movement, the Vietnam War, and what we called then "Women's Liberation." (That King Kong's massive physical body lacks, for all we can tell, an appropriate—um—part—to advance his unusual romantic life, is a fact activists would explore in the coming revolutionary age.) In addition to shifting roles for men and women, there were changes in how families are understood, in relationships between children and adults, in the responsibilities of individuals and communities.

Oscar and I experienced one element of radical change in those times when Carol announced she had other plans than going to college. And then her older brother, Louis, began to talk about becoming a priest. Curtis was the one who gave us comfort by staying with his first choice of career. (That plan, though, was later delayed by war.)

Still, all has turned out well. In fact, I had a wonderful crowd of children, grandchildren, and great grandchildren to help me celebrate my birthday this past weekend. So, when I turn the Cracker Jack toy of my memory at an angle, I see the new opportunities and new challenges my children encountered in the next quarter of a century.

It's a little like peering though Lewis Carroll's looking glass. I'd read that book and Carroll's earlier *Alice's Adventures in Wonderland*. *Through the Looking Glass* is a kind of inversion of the first story: set in winter rather than spring; featuring changes in place rather than in size; linked to chess rather than card games.

"Lewis Carroll" was, of course, the pen name of Charles Dodgson, by profession a mathematician. He wrote down his fantasies, some believe, as entertainment for a little girl and perhaps as an escape from the logical rigors of numbers. So, his personality resembles a lenticular image--pure rationality and nonsense in one package.

Noting that his most famous book was published in 1865, I feel I must have looked in some sort of magical window myself about a century later, close to my 50th birthday. Now, only two years short of the century mark, I am, according to my doctors, "in sound health" (for my age!). So, the sense I had back then that my life was turning a corner is more meaningful than I knew. I was entering the second half (at least) of a long, long life.

At the time, though, I was not ready for a mid-life crisis. Generally, such rebellions were expected of men, not women, anyway. And Oscar certainly faced temptation in the form of "Little Sheba" as he approached middle age. But a quiet discontent was sneaking up on me, too.

At the time I fussed about the re-routing of traffic in and around Fairfield required to accommodate the completion of Interstate 44, the highway that replaced famous Route 66: new feeder roads built, old streets made one-way, traffic lights added, and the fundamental shape of the town redesigned. We had to adjust to a faster pace of life in a more complex system.

There's a satisfaction in recalling the decision that changed the direction of my life, now referred to fondly by my family as "Utility-ization." I simply co-opted space in our new house as a place where I could read, knit, and start my own little business. That event, though, not unlike the Cracker Jack toy, had positive and negative components, as you are about to learn.

# Volume I: Pond

# Chapter One: Boxes

In her mind Mid could hear Oscar saying, *"Come in or go out; go in or come out."*

When anyone in the family opened a door but hesitated to go through it, that's what they heard. Hard times in his childhood--and early in their marriage--made Oscar feel that, in such situations, heat would be coming in or going out--and that cost money.

Mid's head and shoulders had emerged into the attic but the rest of her was still on the ladder in the garage when she heard her son's motor scooter coming up the hill. The sound caused her to pause and then to imagine her husband issuing his customary demand.

She knew the engine sound belonged to Curtis because the muffler on his half-Cushman/half-Allstate aged vehicle was shot. This was a greater source of irritation to their neighbors, she would later learn, than she knew at the time. Right now the interruption seemed one more sign that she was doomed this summer to take at least one step back for every step forward.

As their last child was preparing to go away to college--that is, when the Lindblooms needed less inside space and fewer outside chores--they had bought a bigger house with more yard. Many their age did the same thing, not seeing the irony. Members of the Greatest Generation were caught up in a cultural swell, and Mid was among the few who saw signs of that wave cresting. She worried that they could be swept back in some kind of undertow.

"Carol," she called down to the kitchen, which connected to the garage off a small landing. "Don't let him get away. We'll need help with the heavy things."

Curtis had gone out for twine to tie up boxes; but Mid knew that he, already being pulled into a summer romance, would be alert for opportunities to escape. Carol called back, "He can take my place." She was boxing up canned goods in the kitchen,

"You stay right where you are," instructed Mid. "His place is the basement with your father's old files." Mid felt Carol was at a difficult time in her life--in the middle of summer after graduation from high school with no regular job and soured on a series of immature boyfriends.

"Where's Mom?" Mid heard Curtis ask his sister.

"I'm in the garage," Mid called out. She had taken several steps down the primitive two-by-four ladder attached to the garage's inner wall. "Give Carol her twine and start on your father's file cabinets. When your brother gets here, he can put hanging clothes in wardrobe boxes." Louis was coming back from law school at St. Louis University to help with the move.

Both her boys, like their father, were susceptible to distraction. Mid couldn't quite understand, in fact, how Louis was doing so well at law school, which

11

required concentration and retention. She believed that Carol was her most reliable child--intensely analytical (according to her math and science teachers), having a nearly photographic memory (claimed her history teacher), and tenacious (said anyone who had ever told her she couldn't do something). Mid would soon be shocked by where these qualities were taking her gifted daughter.

Predicting that she and three children would apply themselves for the rest of this Saturday and into the week, Mid had optimistically envisioned an orderly transition to their spacious new residence across town. She had already packed up many valuables: the silver, her jewelry, Oscar's fine watches and fountain pens, and her one Lacy family heirloom (an irregularly functioning marble mantel clock). They were locked in the trunk of her car.

She had asked Oscar, who was teaching summer school, to come home at lunchtime and help supervise for half the day. Sent off into reverie at any treasure from the past, though, Oscar would have trouble parting with any of his college papers--lab reports, radio scripts, architectural drawings. They needed to be taken from their heavy metal file cabinets, boxed, and hauled up from the basement. Over the years Mid had shoved the Army-surplus, olive drab monstrosities deeper and deeper into the basement. Her ultimate goal was to sink them in the Gasconade River.

Movers would come on Wednesday, take furniture, appliances, and the heavy things that had been packed to the new home on Middlecourt Lane.

12

The family--all those Mid could keep around--would bring the loose items and clean up after that. Mid's chore right now was the attic. Fifteen years worth of her children's old clothes, outdated home furnishings, toys, and school projects had to be brought down and arranged for moving or disposal.

She admitted privately that she could woolgather herself while knitting or on her daily walks down to Crystal Pond; but, having come to her role of competent housekeeper after nearly a decade working as a medical technologist, she could maintain concentration when necessary. At that time she had gone back to using her full name, Marian. Her siblings had changed it to "Mid," because she was between older brother and sister and younger brother and sister.

"Mom! Shouldn't you be wearing slacks up there?" Carol, having escorted Curtis across the landing and down the stairs to the basement, now stood in the doorway to the garage. She must have noticed Mid's bare calves.

"I meant to move right on up the ladder, but then I realized I had to keep an eye on you and your brother. And you know a housecoat is perfectly proper for a woman doing chores at home. Oh, by the way: come in or go out; go in or come out."

She scowled at the jeans Carol was wearing. She sometimes washed them in hot water and let them shrink to her shape. Carol scowled back at the loose garment her mother had on, probably happy only that it had a zipper up the front rather than a sash to hold it closed. Although the two women could see their resemblance in a mirror, they were conspicuously divided by a fashion gap. And by an odd combination of rivalry and mutual admiration.

"Well, so long as you're out here by yourself— " conceded Carol. "Say, Mom, before you do disappear into the museum up there—" she gestured. "Can I ask you something?"

"Sure." Mid half turned to look down at her.

"Before you met Dad, during the war, you were overseas for a time."

"Yes, but it was a short period, where they needed a medical technologist." This was true, though Mid did not in the end serve in that professional capacity.

"Was it difficult, being away from home and family?"

"Everyone had a hard time, then, honey. Sure I missed my family, but what was happening all around me made that a minor worry. The bombers flew every day, and the wounded came in faster than we could take care of them."

Carol unconsciously stroked the outside of the ladder with one hand. "And where exactly were you? What were you doing? You weren't a nurse dealing directly with patients."

Mid paused. "You know your Dad doesn't like me to talk about that time."

"But he didn't know you yet. Why does it matter _ if you explain what you were doing?"

14

Mid looked hard at her and then climbed down the ladder to the garage floor. ("*A few more steps backward*," she thought to herself.) To Carol she said, "That was an agreement we made, to move forward rather than backward. His career was on hold after his graduation from Salinas Wesleyan. If his parents-- Grandpa and Grandma--hadn't had some health problems, he would have gone to graduate school right away. Meanwhile, I was—seeing all I wanted to see of war. So, we—we said we were not going to linger on that. We would start our story in the spring of '43, when we met."

Carol nodded. "Had the draft started yet?"

"Yes, and your dad did think he'd have to go into the Army. A lot of boys started signing up after Pearl Harbor, of course."

"But he was turned down, wasn't he? His eyesight."

"Yes, twice. But, the demand was so great that after a while, standards were lowered and he believed it was only a matter of time. Every able-bodied male was needed."

Mid thought about Oscar's music instructor and friend, so talented but so quickly killed in training. Then there was Tony Giordano, her first love, dead in combat on African sands. "But why are you asking about all this today?"

"Oh, I was reading about women in World War II, all those nurses that volunteered. It was such a brave thing to do." She turned to go back to the kitchen and then added, "But it helped free them from the home, from miserable lives."

"Hey! Our lives weren't miserable then, and mine isn't now. Don't you go believing everything you hear about how we were oppressed." She turned to resume her climb. "Anyway, if you wanted women to be more liberated, you shouldn't worry if I show my legs now and then."

Mid didn't want to admit to herself that she wished Oscar might pass by, look up her skirt, and get excited. Yes, she knew she was fifty (-ish). And, though some years younger himself, Oscar still professed to find her attractive. She recalled the last time they had felt in the mood. Poised above her, he had hesitated, a faraway look of abstraction taking possession of his face. Pulling him closer, she had whispered, *"Come in or go out; go in or come out!"*

# Chapter Two: Shifts

In the attic Mid studied the stacks of boxes in varying sizes at irregular heights. When she lay the work light on the floor, its cord snaking back down to an outlet in the garage, the enlarged shadows on the slanted ceiling made her task seem doubly difficult. *"It's the New York City skyline,"* she thought to herself, recalling the view she'd had from her childhood Rutherford home. *"Am I going forward or backward in time?"*

This storage area was only one-third of the attic. The rest had been converted to a large bedroom and a three-quarter's bath for the boys. Carol had the small, second bedroom on the ground floor, while Oscar's office was tucked into a finished portion of the basement at the bottom of the stairs. Mid's plan for the day was to make a quick inventory, label each box "move" or "throw away," and allow no review of her actions.

As she worked, she fretted about Carol's questions. When she was her daughter's age, she had admired those who were eager to take action, especially as fascism spread in Europe. Later, frustrated at the limitations she faced working near her home in New Jersey and recognizing the growing national need, she had decided to join the wartime effort.

However, returning from those months abroad, she realized that the costs of war she witnessed had changed her forever. She didn't want her daughter to think such a course was attractive, especially in this new war in Vietnam. Like many, she had been in favor of it initially, but the more she learned, the more she feared a Korea-style stalemate. She was pleased her sons were safe from the draft so long as they were in school. And both had adopted their father's conviction that superior minds should be used where they could help the most--*not* in combat.

Oscar had always been proud of his wartime research work for the Navy. His father, who had served in the Swedish military, had strongly opposed Oscar's enlisting as a soldier. His mother was equally adamant, having had a brother invalided in the first World War. But, in the end, it was Oscar who chose his own path and convinced Mid it was the right one. He insisted that the day he took the Army physical provided all the evidence necessary to prove his point.

"I wasn't supposed to be looking, of course," he told his bride of three months. "But, my head was down and I could see back between my legs."

Two rows of recruits had reached the hemorrhoid inspection of the examination process; so, their shorts down, they were told to bend over and, explained Oscar, "spread them. Those guys were upside down in my view, but I knew I was looking at a row of butts."

Mid giggled because he was being bold in telling her. In her medical training, however, she had learned how to view the human body objectively. She could stick a finger for blood, take the temperature of an unconscious patient, measure the size of a tumorous organ.

"Did you think, 'cannon fodder'?" she asked. "Or ass-backwards?"

"Not exactly. I thought what they say about Fords: 'everybody's got one.'"

"Hah!"

"And I concluded that other parts of Oscar Lindbloom had more to offer the nation than—a hole."

"It's good that they turned you down, at least for now."

"Yes, but I think I'd better follow up on Professor Peer's recommendation. They need scientists for weapons research. It will mean putting off my plans for graduate school, but it might even be that work experience helps me later on."

Mid and Oscar had eloped the previous spring, letting their families--her mother in Kansas and his parents in New Jersey--know several days later with phone calls. Because the nation was, many felt, on the brink of war, a speedy marriage was not uncommon. And they promised to bring their spouses for visits as soon as it was possible.

The couple concluded that the day of his physical examination was a pivotal moment in their shared journey; they would look forward and back to determine their course rather than automatically follow the masses. Their goal was to survive and live productive lives in a new era.

In the attic, Mid heard Curtis call from the garage floor, "Did anyone phone while I was gone? I—uh— may need to go out later."

"Are you asking if the Survey has your employment status straightened out or if Sarah wants you to come down to Newtown and—sort menus with her."

"Now, Mom, she's a nice girl, and sometimes she does need help at the restaurant."

Sarah Bridges, a high school senior in the fall, had moved to the area from California, where, according to the news, there were no limits to the behavior of young people. Curtis had gone over to the Turntable on a few evenings, supposedly to help Sarah set up for the next day. Mid wanted her son looking forward to the women he would see again at Westminster in the fall, not back to a younger girl whose highest ambition was probably to be a hair dresser.

"No calls," Mid yelled back. "You work for me right now, not the Survey or the Turntable."

Curtis had been given a summer job with the Missouri Geological Survey, doing fieldwork on well-digging and placement. But there had been some glitch in what budget line he was assigned to, so his official starting date had been pushed back a week. He felt he was treading water in his drive to earn enough money to buy his own car; but Mid saw the delay as convenient because he could help with the move at a crucial point.

"Who do I work for?" called Oscar from the garage. "Am I upstairs or downstairs help?"

Mid smiled. "You report to me, of course. I've got boxes, and boxes, and more boxes that need to come down from here and be stacked in an orderly fashion on the garage floor."

"I'll be right up after I put these papers in my office." Mid was about to object, fearing he would be distracted by things on his desk, or in his briefcase, or in his mind. But then he added, "And I have something to tell you"; so she concluded he would stay on course.

Keeping an ear out for him, she shoved three more boxes--labeled "Throw Away," "Throw Away," "Move"--close to the trapdoor entrance. The third box contained letters, ironically--given Carol's questions-- some of them written or received when she was overseas. She knew if she opened them and started reading, she'd be pulled back into another time, a former serious romance. And that wartime experience she wanted to keep from her daughter.

Oscar's head appeared in the trapdoor. "Hi, Sarge." He liked to use that nickname for Mid on the rare occasions he was pulled into household chores. "Guess what?"

"I'll guess your news after you guess your assignment."

"It looks to me as if these go to the trash." He gestured. "And these to the staging area."

"Very good. You'll have more in each category soon. So, what's new at South Central Missouri State University?" The recent change from the "School of Mines and Metallurgy" to university status was forward-looking to some, but others regretted it as a departure from their history as a small college.

"Well, you know the new chancellor wants to promote the arts as we try to recruit more women and build new programs."

Mid grumbled. "It'd be good for the whole town if there were more women around."

"I don't know about that, but, anyway, the new theater program is planning to put on two plays each semester next year. And they need volunteers."

Oscar had acted in several productions when he was a student at Salinas Wesleyan, and he'd had success writing scripts for radio dramas that aired on the local station.

"So, you're going to write for them? Reveal the hidden talent of the physicist known for his study of liquids?"

"I might do that. But right now they need a director for *Come Back, Little Sheba*."

"That's wonderful, dear! By the time you have to get busy, we'll be done with this move. Oh, and by the way, have you made a final decision about your father's old desk?" Carl had built a classic roll-top desk Oscar kept in his study but didn't use.

"Ah, yes. Let's at least put it in the utility room for now." He looked at the boxes. "Oh, I should say — um — the person in charge, the new faculty member, would like me to start making some preparations before then — if possible." He trailed off, then began energetically shifting boxes to take down the ladder.

Mid stood with one hand on her hip. "And just who is this person?"

"Ah, yes. It's, um, that new woman, Professor Baudin."

Somehow, Mid knew she was the one. The strikingly attractive young blonde had been the talk of the campus when she came to interview back in the spring. And Mid knew that, although he would never admit it (because she herself was a brunette), Oscar preferred blondes.

# Chapter Three: Inversions

Mid looked at her reflection in Crystal Pond and thought of the two women in *Come Back, Little Sheba*-- the mature, unhappy Lola, married and childless; and the attractive, young Marie who enjoys two beaus. Lola mourns her dog, Sheba, who ran away; but it's clear she feels innocence and joy have escaped her, too. Was Mid somewhere between these two?

She pitched a small stone into the pond and watched the ripple spread out from the splash. She had slipped away from the house after dinner and the dishes to spend a few moments at her favorite site for reflection. Crystal Pond was just one hundred yards off of Limestone Drive. Three houses west of the Lindblooms', a path began in an empty lot and wound down the hill through some woods to the pond's edge.

When she had proposed moving to a new house across town, she hoped it might inspire other changes, including more involvement in Fairfield cultural events. Carol would be up in Columbia by the fall, after all, and both boys back to their schools. A tenured full professor, Oscar should have more free time. Was he going to use this freedom apart from her?

Because the land sloped away beyond the pond, Mid could look across the water and see the sun hovering above the distant horizon. No one seemed to know who owned the lot on Limestone and the land around the pond; but the area had become an unofficial park for children and adults. Mid came here when she could, perhaps because, though much smaller, it reminded her of Greenwood Lake, where her family had camped when she was a child in New Jersey.

She loved the outdoors. Oscar claimed to as well, but more often choose to stay in and read a book or lose himself in whatever it is that theoretical physicists think about. Mid wondered if he was thinking about Marsha Baudin.

"So that's where you got to. I guessed correctly."

"Ah, Louis," Mid said, starting but not turning around. She correctly surmised that this was her older son and that he had used the analytical skills he was refining in law school to find her. Because of the stillness of the water, she could see a reflection of him come up beside her.

"Look at what I discovered," he said, holding up a black rectangular box.

"The pinhole camera your uncle bought you! I thought we'd thrown those away."

Mid's younger brother, who had been an airplane mechanic during the war, had surprised the rest of the family by going into the ministry and, even more, by taking a black church in Louisville, KY. He was always struggling financially and sometimes took on extra work--like selling box camera kits--to supplement the family income.

Louis turned the camera in the sunlight. "I loved this, maybe one of the best, unexpected presents we ever got." This was characteristic of him, the child who respected his elders. It was easy for Mid to feel proud of him. He could be counted on, at least more than his brother.

Uncle Bill had come to see the Lindblooms when they were spending a summer at Oak Ridge National Laboratory in Tennessee. Oscar's research there would help toward his promotion, but Marian had had to devise projects to keep the kids entertained, as they knew so few people there. The camera kits had served well for a few weeks, especially with Louis.

"You were old enough to appreciate it, but the other two didn't have the patience."

Louis laughed. "Curtis might have done better in his physics class this year if he'd paid more attention to the principles of light." His younger brother had bragged that he passed physics (taken in large part to please his father) but admitted he enjoyed his English classes a lot more.

"Right. It's so simple." Mid took the camera from Louis and pointed it over the pond. "The rays pass through the lens. Well, the pin-hole--there's not even a real lens--and then projects an inverted picture on the film."

She could see a miniature version of what she was aiming at in a small rectangular window on the top of the camera. A tiny mirror reflected what was visible in front of her through the tiny window in the front. The shutter was opened by depressing a small red lever on the side of the black box. When she pushed it, she heard a familiar, two-syllable click.

"Presto, a photograph!" Louis announced.

"A photograph if you hold the camera still enough and time the exposure accurately." She handed it back to him.

"Have you saved any of your old photos? I think you took more than all three of us."

Mid had always wanted to paint. Her work in college and in medical labs had required that she draw meticulous diagrams of what she saw in microscopes; and she took pride in accuracy. But there was no room for her individual touch in such work. That summer in Tennessee she was imagining using photographs as models for more expressive watercolors.

"I'm afraid not. Part of the goal of moving is to discard things we don't really need."

"Ah, make room for new projects. Hmm, maybe you'll go back to work as Carol starts college. You'll have a lot more free time."

"I really haven't thought that far ahead. I had hoped—well, it's hard to predict."

"Maybe I should use this to record the beginning of a new phase," laughed Louis, aiming the camera across the pond and then back at his mother. "Smile!"

She scowled. The camera made her remember that, when her brother Will had visited them at Oak Ridge, he'd also carried the fine mantle clock their father had loved. Now, with the pendulum removed and the works stopped, it was carefully packed in a wooden crate. It would be cleaned and adjusted before put in place in the new house. She treasured it because it came from her father, now dead nearly thirty years.

"What do *you* see in your future, second year law student? A love interest among any of your classmates?"

Now it was his turn to scowl. "Most of the class are men, of course. And the few women they let in are so, sooo serious."

"Maybe off campus, then. You know a lot depends on where you look. Again, your camera can teach the lesson." She held it up. "The smaller the pinhole, the sharper the image; but clarity is also affected by distance."

"Please explain how that applies to me, professor. Also, spare me from a lecture from Carol later or a story from Dad about he never had a camera when he was a boy. Why, he and his friends would make a fist, I bet, squint through a gap between the thumb and forefinger, and pretend they had taken a picture!"

"Ha! You know him well. So, the smaller the hole--the *aperture*--the sharper the image, but that image is dimmer because there's less light. So, if you're focusing narrowly to find the one woman who would appeal to you, her image might be too dim for you to see."

"Hmm. If I broaden the focus, a different pattern must be discovered?"

"Yes. If you're taking a big look at all of St. Louis, widening your frame of vision, maybe someone's face will jump out as clear as if you'd been seen it in a vision."

"Or the frog prince coming up to the surface of the princess' pond? Did you spot Dad in all of Jefferson City by figuring your future husband could be anywhere?"

"You won't believe this, but I already had a picture of him in mind, and he of me."

Louis gazed out over the pond. "You know, I did meet a kind of interesting girl — "

"There's a 'but' here. Go on."

"Well, I went to a mixer at Fontbonne. They had a nice little jazz combo, and I struck up a conversation with a senior who was thinking of going to law school."

"Fontbonne is a Catholic girls' school, isn't it?"

"Right. So, no real future there." But Mid heard this assertion as possibly a question.

"Yes. Becoming Catholic might be as bad as becoming a missionary like your uncle."

Mid had insisted her children attend a Baptist Sunday school; but, because Oscar refused to have anything to do with formal church, none of the three took a genuine interest. They did absorb the idea that Catholicism was a different religion. And if any of them wanted to pursue a relationship with a Catholic, it was understood he or she would have to convert.

This was the most visible social division in Fairfield, as St. Stephens had its own school through eighth grade. There were, in fact, a small number of black families living in town and in the county; but unless whites played sports, which neither of Lindbloom boys did, children from different races had little interaction.

Mid clucked her tongue. "Come on. Let's get back to the house and focus on the here and now rather than the what might be in the future."

Over the years, whenever she replayed this moment in memory, she realized she'd not seen what might be in the future, but what was to be.

# Chapter Four: Agents

Back at the house, Mid found Oscar and Carol in the living room watching *The Man from U.N.C.L.E.* She sent Louis upstairs as a spy (like Napoleon Solo) to see if he could determine how serious Curtis' summer romance with Sarah Bridges might be.

She went on to her bedroom, intending to add a few rows to the baby sweater she was knitting to sell at the hospital gift shop. She also had to go through Oscar's shirts to see which had too many tiny burn holes caused by his pipe. When she'd married him, he smoked cigarettes like most men. In his second year in Fairfield, he'd given them up for a pipe. Mid found both habits a nuisance--and costly in terms of ruined shirts.

On the little bench at her dressing table, she sat for a moment to review the day. A lot had gotten done; and she was pleased to have all the family around her. Still, the woman she was inspecting in the mirror looked oddly alone.

"No children in the house this fall," she thought to herself. "I'll miss them, of course, and all we've done together the past twenty years; but this is also an opportunity for me."

She remembered when she'd been on her own after college, working as a medical technologist in her home state of New Jersey. She shared a small country house with her mother, so she had company when she wanted it but freedom at the same time. On the weekend, she could take a train into New York City and see the sights, even if she couldn't afford expensive entertainment. In the bright lights and hurried pace of Manhattan she anticipated a future of bold action in faraway places.

That pre-war time of high hope now seemed more remote than her childhood, which had been spent in a busy domestic environment of four siblings, two grandparents (one paternal, one maternal), and her parents in a large house on Ridge Road in Rutherford. She had recreated similar conditions--if on a slightly smaller scale--raising three children in a neighborhood with many young families (as well as seeing after Oscar's parents in nearby Jefferson City).

Soon, though, she'd be alone in a big house in a strange neighborhood with an absent-minded husband who resembled Mid's own mother in widowhood. The latter wrote poetry and read the Bible; this one spent his evening alternating between theoretical physics and fantastic adventures in books or on television.

She wandered back to the living rooms and saw that Napoleon Solo (Robert Vaughn) was entering Del Floria's Tailor Shop, where he could disappear through a secret entrance and reappear in U.N.C.L.E. headquarters. Mid knew her husband liked the show's abrupt transitions from ordinary life into a world of adventure, plain men suddenly becoming agents dedicated to stopping plots by their THRUSH counterparts, also disguised as ordinary citizens.

"What's going on?" she asked.

"Shhh!" Oscar hated it when others talked during a show, insisting they wait for commercials. But Carol gestured to her mother to come close. "It's another episode with Eve Poole," she whispered as Mid joined her on the sofa. "We think she's a double agent this time." The willowy actress had made several appearances in the series as a seductive operative for America's enemies.

"Is she that blonde in the raincoat?" Mid whispered back, noting a woman studying the clothes in the store window--or perhaps trying to see beyond them to what was going on inside the shop. Mapping the enemy's headquarters was always an agent's goal.

"Yes. She's taking pictures with a miniature camera in her handbag."

"Clever!" Viewers could see Eve's back directly and view her face reflected in the window. Mid guessed the pictures she was taking would quickly circulate throughout THRUSH.

"Yes, she's like you, Mom, coordinating a staff of disguised operatives to take apart one house and reassemble it in another location." She patted her mother's arm." You, of course--you're a *re-doubled* agent, one of the good guys."

The episode paused for a Chevrolet commercial featuring the show's star, Robert Vaughn. Mid was going to mention the recovered pinhole camera, but Oscar again gestured for quiet. He loved cars and wanted to hear about the new Corvair, "automobile of the future," according to the man from U.N.C.L.E.

"Ha!" he laughed. A longtime subscriber to *Road and Track*, he kept up with industry news. "They've already shown the car is unsafe. Stick with Nashes."

"So I get to keep my little Rambler instead of trading for a Corvair?"

She loved her boxy, plain, vehicle, joking that it was deliberately designed so that you couldn't tell which was the hood or trunk and thus whether it was about to go forward or backwards. "The most versatile car there is," she asserted.

"You get to keep it so long as Curtis doesn't borrow it to sneak down to Newtown," laughed Carol, who seldom needed either family car, walking or biking wherever she need to go, concentrating on her fitness for softball. Louis was happy with his own used but reliable VW Beetle, which, with the engine in the trunk, seemed to have been built backwards.

"That reminds me—" Mid said, glancing toward the stairs up to the boys' room. What was Louis learning? It could be a difficult summer if she had to watch Curtis indulge in a fling that was doomed to end in September. She knew herself how vulnerable young girls can be.

The show resumed with Eve Poole's character, agent Dromio, gazing intently into the eyes of a distinguished older man on some formal occasion, perhaps a gathering of diplomats and ambassadors in what might be a receiving room at the White House.

Carol whispered that the gentleman was, in fact, the Vice President of the United States, who, unknown to the rest of the country, temporarily had control of the red telephone that could launch a nuclear attack. The President had had to have emergency surgery to remove his appendix--or, that's what the THRUSH agents had made his doctors believe; and the acting commander-in-chief felt it was important to keep to his posted schedule by attending the reception.

Carol pulled her mother closer. "I kind of like her, even if she's on the wrong side."

"Oh? How she uses her feminine charms?"

"No, not that so much. She gets tough when the situation requires it. Watch. I bet she's going to take action."

Double agent Dromio signaled another female agent on the ballroom balcony.

"Uh-oh, looks like her twin up there," Mid whispered.

"You're right, played by Eve, though--trick camera work and a body double. Look!"

The balcony spy had pulled a small mirror from her handbag and was shining it into the eyes of a man standing beside the Vice President. He doubled over in pain, more than would make sense under ordinary circumstances.

"He's one of our guys, bodyguard. His eyes are super sensitive after being exposed to some weird kind of radiation," Carol explained.

When the secret service agent collapsed, drawing everyone's attention, the floor-Dromio took out another guard with a kick to the knee and a karate chop to the back of the neck. Grabbing his gun, she fired several shots into the air. Her balcony twin dropped a smoke grenade down into the crowd, and pandemonium broke out.

Mid was beginning to lose interest, confident that order would be restored as always in the land of television. But, she wondered: was her world moving toward a new order or a new chaos? Would she be at peace in her new home or restless to do more on her own?Was this the beginning of a new phase in her life or simply a continuation of the old one?

Her mind drifted back to cars, to the independence the two-year old Rambler gave her. Before the second family car, she'd had to schedule trips to town on a fixed weekday afternoon or on weekends. Having grown up poor, Oscar felt a car represented one's status. And Mid understood that it gave him pleasure to see eyes turn when he stepped out of a car unlike any other in the faculty parking lot.

He made his first statement (when he was promoted to associate professor) with a 1951 Nash Ambassador. That car did not survive a collision in Pennsylvania-- thankfully, the family did; and it was followed by the 1955 model. His current prize, a 1960 Jaguar 3.4 sedan, was even more distinctive, though

Mid could not understand why no mechanic in Fairfield, Jefferson City, or St. Louis could fix the slow oil leak that spotted the garage floor.

When the phone rang, Mid jumped up. Before she could answer, another voice from the upstairs extension was speaking. She paused just long enough before hanging up to hear Curtis say to someone (Sarah Bridges?), "I'll be there with—*something to drink*." His last words were whispered. *Oh, dear*, thought Mid: *yet another worry*.

# Chapter Five: Opposites

"What are we going to do about this?" Mid asked Oscar as they got ready for bed. "I'm sure he's taking alcohol to a minor!"

Oscar was inspecting his shirt to see if it could be worn another day. Having his shirts done at the laundry was, according to him, a gift to Mid, although it was also a second confirmation that he'd reached the professional status for which his parents sacrificed. "You don't know that. And it's probably just beer. He's been to college, Mid; what do you expect?"

"I expect my children to behave the way — the way we did when we were young."

To herself she admitted that she meant back when they had been in college. After that — well, she had her bottles of wine and a few romantic entanglements that went further than was completely proper. But don't we all edit our pasts when directing our children's future?

"Curtis will be okay. Why don't you worry about Louis? He's out of college and seems to have no interest in finding the right girl for him." Like most in his generation, Oscar believed marriage stabilized a man and made him productive.

Mid pulled back the covers and prepared to get in. "He told me today that he has his eyes open; he's looking." She flapped the sheet a few times to create a breeze. "Is the fan on high?"

They had a powerful exhaust fan in the attic, which kept the house cool on all but the hottest nights. Well, the downstairs was always comfortable, but the boys regularly proposed their parents change bedrooms with them and see how the other half lived.

"Fan is on."

"I don't know anything about this Sarah Bridges girl. Why is she working over in Newtown? Is that where she lives?"

Newtown was an old railroad town ten miles west of Fairfield, important during the war; but its glory days were in the past and its future was grim. Train crews and passengers used to stay at a fine hotel built by the train company (now closed) and eat at the Turntable, which hung on only because long-time residents preferred old-fashioned country cooking to the newer, fast-food places that seemed to be taking over Fairfield and the nation.

Oscar didn't answer, and Mid knew he'd drifted away from her concerns as easily as she'd slipped off from *The Man from U.N.C.L.E.* He could already be dreaming of Eve Poole—or Marsha Baudin.

It occurred to her that Sarah might be from a military family stationed at Fort Leonard Wood but living in Phipps County in order to take advantage of the schools. If so, she'd be close to Newtown, and it might make sense that she worked there. But, an Army brat, this girl would have seen more of the world at a young age than her son.

Why did her children seem so naive to the ways of the world? Their father had been more innocent than she expected back when he courted Mid. Of course, she was some years older and had traveled more. Plus, he was a true romantic. But those are not inherited traits!

Perhaps this age's social convention of never discussing unpleasant topics--adultery, for instance-- had its drawbacks. Mid knew not all husbands were like television's Dick Van Dyke in his devotion to Mary Tyler Moore; but that Fairfield had its own *Peyton Place* incidents was never dinner topic conversation at the Lindblooms. She would not, for instance, tell her daughter that Arthur James, attractive widower, had flirted with her at the last departmental social.

The scene could even have gotten out of hand had Oscar come upon them. The two men belonged in different camps--the experimentalists and the theoretical physicists. Most of the time this rivalry involved harmless banter. Arthur had been overheard claiming that some of his colleagues spent far too much time playing with "imaginary" numbers (aware, of course, that imaginary numbers are sound mathematical units with concrete application in science and engineering). For his part, Oscar confided to one friend that, with two first names, one could never tell whether "James Arthur" was coming or going. But discussion of the proper allocation of research funds and teaching assignments could be more acrimonious.

James' suggestive comments to Mid were not the only disquieting part of the department's annual summer picnic, held on the department chair Harold Miller's twenty-acre farm just east of town. This was usually a happy occasion, as the pace would now slow both for those teaching summer school and for those engaged in research projects. But this time Mid had felt an undercurrent of anxiety in the informal conversation before dinner.

After a quiet first year observing the institution, a new chancellor was starting to make his presence felt. Would he remain true to the school's tradition as a small college with an emphasis on teaching or push them toward becoming a research institution with heavy emphasis on getting grants and establishing ties with industry? When he came to Fairfield after the war, Professor Miller had deliberately recruited Ph.D.'s to replace retiring faculty with master's degrees, perhaps anticipating the institution's achieving university status. (That had become official the previous year.) He would probably be in favor of change.

"You know, it's a shame your husband doesn't think much of experimentalists," Arthur James said to Mid as she was setting her apple pie on the dessert table.

"Is that right? We wives don't understand all that—that science you men do."

Contributions to the pot-luck event reflected the faculty wives' varied cooking styles and their husbands' tastes. This was the first year, though, that they had a vegetarian, Professor Johnson's wife, a Californian. Many worried that she'd object to the hamburgers and hot dogs grilled for the occasion. While they noticed the popularity of trends like Weight Watchers, little did any of the meat-and-potatoes Midwesterners foresee the coming of such things as the extra-low-calorie, no gluten, or vegan diets.

Professor James looked again at Mid's dish. "Beautiful ratio of a circle's circumference to its diameter!"

"Ah, you mean 'pie.'"

"Yes. I figured you were one of the women who really do understand science. Of course, a lot of us have problems with the social sciences--psychology, sociology, the newer disciplines."

Mid was looking for a group to join and leave this man behind, but he seemed to end up in her view whichever way she looked.

"I like to study how opposites attract, contradicting the law of affinities." He noted. "Quarks may prove one of my theories."

"Quarks?"

"Subatomic articles with flavor, charm, bottomness, topness." He stepped back and ran his eyes up and down Mid's figure. "If we were all quarks, now, I'd say there are such very fine bottomnesses and topnesses at this event that I can envision a revealing experiment."

Fortunately at that moment, Charlotte Miller, wife of the department chair, appeared at Mid's elbow, insisting that she had to talk about the week's bridge schedule. "That man," said Charlotte. "I know he's sad, but someone might have to black his eyes for him."

Mid thought Oscar might be the one to do it. Her husband, like many Scandinavians, appeared cool on the outside; but he had a temper that could erupt with little notice. And from stories he'd told her about growing up, he tended to win scraps with his rivals.

Now, James was a good looking man, and he wanted to please. The women especially felt sorry for him when he arrived in town three years after his wife died of cancer. They understood his desire for companionship, but many felt he was needy and carelessly forward in conversation. An amateur magician, for instance, he tried too hard to impress women by making objects disappear from one place (his hand), reappear in another (their hair).

"You know," said Oscar that night, turning on his side and looking at Mid. Lost in her reverie, she almost jumped. "I may have met this Bridges' girl's father--Colonel Bridges, retired, now teaching mechanical engineering. He said he had two children, one still in high school."

Mid had been replaying her conversation with Oscar's colleague, admitting that attention from a man was sometimes welcome.

"Oh? What's he like?"

"He seems pleasant enough, though—"

"Though what?"

"Well, he's—um—Afro-American, I think. Not real dark and he doesn't have all the usual features."

Whoa! Did this mean her young son was dating a black girl? And was her older boy interested in a Catholic? Her husband was getting ready to collaborate with a blonde bombshell in the drama department, and she was fending off a lusty widower. What was her world coming to? At least she, she concluded, she could count on her sober and determined daughter!

# Chapter Six: Turns

"I'm going to enlist in the Army," Carol said on Monday.

Oscar and Mid, standing in the hall outside the bathroom and between the two bedrooms, could find nothing to say. They had stopped in the middle of the house while sliding a cardboard wardrobe box toward the dining room, the indoor staging area for the move.

Carol smiled, as if she had just delivered welcome news to her parents. "I've been thinking it over, and this will give me good experience, plus pay for my college later." She'd paused from the task Mid had given her--developing a list of which boxes to unpack in what order. Mid wanted the basics in place quickly so they could function immediately in the new house. (She would look back sadly disappointed, however, by the weekend.)

"You have a tuition scholarship to the university already," Mid finally managed. "And we have the money to pay for your housing. Everything's set." Her mind was entertaining the possibility of opening the boxes stacked here and in the garage, returning everything to its former place, and moving clocks back to a time when this wasn't happening.

"I know, but you're still helping Louis with law school, and Curtis has taken a part-time job to help pay his way. You guys deserve to do some of the things you like now that you're—now that you don't have to worry about us."

The world is completely topsy-turvy, thought Mid: our children are now assessing our needs and taking care of us. When did the family turn that corner?

"I don't think this is a good idea, honey," Oscar said, studying the phone on the hall table, as if he were anticipating a call that might remedy the situation. Mid imagined possible messages: *Sorry, your daughter flunked the physical. Turns out we've reached our quota. She's a no-go. The war is over, and we anticipate several centuries of peace.*

Carol went on. "Now, Dad, you've told us—many times—about having to work your way through school at the shoe store and how graduate school had to be put on hold so you could help your parents. I would just be doing what you did, earning my own money for college. And, well, I want to see some of the world, like Mom did."

Mid saw Oscar scowl. She shouldn't have told Carol as much as she had about her past. "But if you go ahead with college now, you'll be able to use your training to travel later. Even if—or *when* you join the military, you'll be telling others what to do, not taking orders. In light of your prospects as an honor student, really, signing up now would be a step backward."

Carol tucked her clipboard under one arm. "I took these tests at the recruiting center. My skills are perfect for what they need in future conflicts."

*Cannon fodder*?" Oscar mouthed to Mid from behind Carol. To their daughter he asked, "Artillery coordinator?"

"They don't send women into the field, Dad. Cryptographers. I have a talent for logic and patterns. Plus I'm good at math, like you. They can guarantee me training in that specialty. And, if I do well in basic, it's likely they'll invite me to consider becoming a WAC officer."

"That means more years of service, though, doesn't it?" said Mid. "You might get on a path with little chance of turning back. And who knows where you could be sent?" She recalled her own time overseas and the fate of several women who'd been Army nurses during the war. Some didn't survive, and others found it difficult to adjust to civilian life later.

"With my study of German, I bet they'll send me to Europe. I'll be eavesdropping over the Iron Curtain." She had visited Curtis at Westminster College last fall and seen where Churchill delivered his famous Iron Curtain speech in 1946. Now Mid was regretting having let her go. Those that learn from history are doomed to repeat it!

She saw Curtis emerge through the kitchen doorway carrying the last empty file cabinet drawer from the basement. Oscar put his shoulder to the wardrobe and announced, "Let's talk about this later. We all need to keep working."

"Talk about what?" Curtis asked, making his way down a narrow lane through stacked boxes. "I must have come in in the middle of something. If she's claiming she has to go work, her next shift is Wednesday. Her life outside the home is on hold for forty-eight hours."

"I didn't say otherwise. But you go to work tomorrow; the Survey called earlier." Putting the clipboard on a stack of boxes, Carol added, "So, it's *your* little romance with Sarah that goes on hold, not my summer without men." She'd declared herself disgusted with the boys she knew and was taking a vow of "spinsterhood" (that's the archaic word she used around her parents--not the equally archaic but more accurate "chastity").

"Romance?" Mid asked, willing to postpone the argument with Carol, which she hadn't seen coming, to engage a problem about which she was far more confident.

"Oh, no romance. Just—friendship. It's not like we've had any dates or anything."

With the Missouri Geological Survey taking him out of Fairfield Monday through Friday, Mid worried that he'd be easy prey for some worldly gold digger on the weekends.

Mid sighed. "Okay, okay. We'll talk about this later, too. Louis is not here to help, so we have a lot to do today and tomorrow."

At one point, she'd had the idea of recording the stages of this carefully planned move with her Kodak Instamatic. Today was to be the end of packing, tomorrow the hauling of small items in their cars over to Middlecourt Lane. Wednesday, middle of the week, was the major turning point with a big truck coming. After that, the arrangement of their earthly possessions in a new house could occur almost leisurely over the rest of the summer. Now, however, her ascent into a comfortable middle age looked more as if it was stalling--or preparing to nosedive.

Though concerned about the men in her family, Mid was just a little bit excited--and oddly proud--of what her daughter was contemplating. Not that she'd ever allow it to happen! But it showed initiative, thinking for herself rather than blindly following a pattern established by others, maybe even guidelines drawn up by her father.

Perhaps she'd resented for some time that Carol wanted to study math and physics like Oscar, not biology and chemistry, as she herself had at Archer College. But she knew Oscar always encouraged Louis and Curtis to pursue their own interests, whatever the field. And he had been as open with Carol, at least in terms of her academic choices.

Still, Mid thought, perhaps somebody else influenced Carol in this unexpected direction. Neither of her brothers had considered military service. In fact, both had ruled out attending their father's university in part because of the required participation in ROTC. She needed to figure out which of Carol's friends had inspired this idea of joining up.

Later, when they were all eating the sandwiches Mid had made ahead of time and frozen, she thought she might have a clue about the source of her daughter's new plan. Carol had launched into a discussion of pinhole cameras. "You know, the technology of this thing goes pretty far back, and not just in Western culture." She was peering into the black box.

Oscar observed, "True. The study of optics is old. Back in the 14th century, Roger Bacon noted that an image is inverted when passing through a tiny aperture."

"Yes, but he was heavily influenced by earlier Arabian philosophers--Alhazen and, before him, Ibn Sahl, who was writing in the 10th century. They had observed sunlight passing through wicker baskets and the resulting shadow patterns. But centuries before Christ, the Chinese identified the optical effect of a pinhole. By the 11th century, they had studied the *camera obscura* and written down laws about its function. We Westerners are kind of late comers to this science."

"Yes," Oscar said. "$d = 2$ times the square root of $f$ times $\lambda$." He knows the formula, thought Mid; but does he see the real life picture of the future Carol is creating?

"That's interesting," Mid asked. "Did you learn this from school or on your own?"

"Well, some of each, but a new friend I've made, an amateur photographer, filled in a lot of the gaps for me. He's seen a lot more of the world than I have."

*Hm,* thought Mid: *Find out who that globetrotting photographer is, and maybe I'll know where these radical ideas of postponing college stem from.* She asked Carol, "Who is that?

"Ah, it's one of Dad's students, actually. He, uh, did his military service before college."

*A-ha!* thought Mid.

Like many parents in Fairfield, Oscar and Mid had opposed their daughter's dating college students while she was in high school. Teenage girls, they insisted, were too easily impressed; and here was proof. But how could they counteract this young man's influence without angering their strong-willed daughter? Mid would have to be tactful. She also knew Oscar could get out of control and harm their cause.

# Chapter Seven: Circles

At the end of week one of the move, Mid proposed she and Oscar go out to eat. "We're bushed, and I've used up all the prepared meals."

"It's going to the Turntable that worries me. You just want to spy on this Bridges girl."

"Don't be silly. The restaurant has good food. Plus, I would get a nice ride in the Jag."

She and the children teased Oscars about his cars, as he kept them meticulously clean and always worried they were going to bring dirt inside or scuff up the upholstery. Whenever they entered or exited, they anticipated his automatic injunction: *Watch your feet!*

"Okay," he conceded. "But we do it this way: come in and take an open table--no scouting out the kitchen, the parking lot, the bathrooms, the building next door, the old railroad yard, the woods across the river. It's in to dinner, out to home."

*Come in or go out; go in or come out,* Mid thought to herself. But she was satisfied. Except on their anniversary, the Lindblooms almost never ate in restaurants.

Something worried her, though, when she slipped into the leather seat of the Jag; but she couldn't quite put her finger on it. Of course, the number of things still left to move from the old house and the disorderly shape of the new one were reasons enough to be unsettled. But she felt there was something else disturbing her.

As they rode west on Interstate 44 (which followed the path of famous Route 66), Mid thought about the old railroad town they were driving to and its railroad turntable, which could reverse a vehicle's direction. Early locomotives were built only to move forward; so when it was necessary to reverse directions, the engineer drove the car onto the large table on a single section of track that lay on the diameter. The table with a 45-ton vehicle on it was rotated 180-degrees so that the locomotive could pull off headed back in the direction from which it had come.

The situation was not that different from the highway traffic circles Mid was familiar with in New Jersey. They irritated Oscar because he sometimes found himself in the wrong lane and having to make several circuits before he could exit in the correct direction. More than once he ended up going back the way he had come.

At the restaurant, Oscar asked, "Did Louis talk to you about law school?"

"Only that he'd be ready for his second year after his summer job at the St. Louis firm. You come out of a clerkship like that and go back to school a step ahead of your classmates."

Mid was scanning the room, wondering if any of the waitresses might be Sarah. Since the staff all wore the restaurant's striped uniform and signature cap of railroad engineers, it was hard to distinguish one from another. When one waitress disappeared through the swinging kitchen doors, Mid couldn't tell if the next one coming out was the same or a different girl.

"Hm," Oscar said. "He was telling me about sampling churches in the big city, like that was what he enjoyed about St. Louis. Why he thought I'd want to know is beyond me."

"You are the philosopher in the family."

"I'm interested in the philosophy of science; and sometimes I even get tired of that."

Mid sensed frustration in Oscar's statement and knew that, having excelled in many fields in college, he sometimes resented being hemmed in with his specialized teaching and research. One of his professors had encouraged him to go on to advanced study in English. And, when Mid first met him, he was playing saxophone in a little Jefferson City jazz combo. Taking on *Come Back, Little Sheba* could, she realized, invigorate him. It would be much better, certainly, than the midlife crisis of red sports car and mistress!

"You might have had more flexibility at another school," mused Mid. He'd once had an offer from a school in Colorado, but Oscar wanted the familiar and to live close to his parents.

"You must be reading my mind. An old friend wrote me about a job in Santa Fe. I'm almost tempted to apply."

Mid came close to spitting out the water she was sipping. "We've just bought a house! We can't up and sell, begin again in another state." For the last two days, she felt the current move, covering a mere mile, was stalled. How much more momentous would be changing jobs!

"Ah, you've always been the bold one, heading west from New Jersey to chart a new course. And we're still young; the kids are mostly on their own." He tapped his finger on his water glass. "There's a fine book by Willa Cather, *The Professor's House*, that makes the desert Southwest intriguing, full of history. I might find new inspiration for my writing or my music."

The conversation was interrupted by the arrival of their food. Mid hoped this idea of a job change was an impulse of the moment, a fantasy he would dream of but not pursue.

As they concentrated on the meal, she surveyed the room again, which was circular like the railroad turntable next door. The restaurant tables were arranged as spokes in a giant wheel, the kitchen a roughly triangular piece of the pie. Through a window they could see the old railroad structure, still occasionally put into operation for train buffs and historical societies.

On the walls were a number of old railroad clocks, reminding Mid that she needed to find someone to clean the Lacy mantle clock. Mr. Agee, at Fairfield Jewelers, had done it for years, but was recently retired. She'd gotten to know him and the procedure for setting the beat on a clock; but more work on it might be needed. Getting the family heirloom up and running in her new house would be a sign for Mid that they had made the transition.

During World War II, with Fort Leonard Wood nearby and military supplies crossing the country on this major east-west route, the Newtown station and turntable were in constant use. Coming here tonight was sort of like going back in time. When the industry switched to new diesel engines, able to travel longer between stops, the operation began to shrink. Everyone suspected that, when Mr. Bachman, whose family had managed the restaurant for over fifty years, retired, the Turntable would close. With the old hotel also gone a decade ago, the town would revert to its original status of a tiny rural community.

As they were finishing their meal, Mid returned the conversation to her elder son. "Maybe it's not so odd that Louis would be trying out churches while in law school. His study is rigorous, some say dull; so he needs different experiences, refueling, I guess."

"Well, in my day, we considered churches primarily as places where girls could be found. Too often, of course, they were the nice ones." Though she later insisted their children have at least a Sunday school education, when she and Oscar met they never discussion religion.

Mid remembered Louis mentioning the Catholic girl at Fontbonne. Had he seen her more than that one time? Had he, like a locomotive brought to a station for repairs, been spun around on a turntable and chugged back to spend more time with her?

She sighed. "Just when I thought everyone in our family was settling down into a comfortable path, all of us are off in different directions. Well, except for me, of course."

"It'll be a lot easier with just me to take care of. You'll have time for flower beds at the new place, and one of the extra bedrooms can be for your knitting." He folded his napkin. "Or maybe you'd like to create a desert garden, fifty species of cacti artfully arranged around bright colored rocks under open skies."

Mid thought of her mother, who, when she became a widow, put in a lovely shade garden under half a dozen backyard fruit trees. Living with her for those first few years after Curtis died, Mid had sometimes felt the little cottage and her mother's devotion to a nearby small church were taking Ethel backwards. She abandoned the poetry she had been publishing in established literary periodicals and lived an increasingly parochial life. Mid didn't want a new house here or elsewhere to be a retreat for her, their move one step forward and two back.

"Dessert?" Oscar asked her, as their waitress approached to clear the dishes.

Looking up, and then past that young woman, Mid saw Curtis by the cash register, bending down and whispering in the ear of a remarkably attractive young woman. Dark hair was sneaking out from under her railroad engineer's cap as he ushered her through the front door, a hand under her elbow. She wished she could go back in time to when he was still a boy and she could intercept him, demand to know his intentions.

"Uh, no. No dessert." She rose and tucked her purse under her arm. "You go ahead and get the bill while I powder my nose."

Sternly addressing the face in the mirror of the ladies room, Mid told herself she could not follow that young couple, even if she spotted her '63 Rambler in the parking lot. Still, she tried to recall the shade of the girl's face as she passed under a light over the door.

When she got back in the Jag, a repressed memory rose up to meet her and scatter her thoughts about Curtis and Sarah Bridges. The scent of an unknown perfume lingered in a car that she assumed never had a female passenger other than herself and her daughter.

# Chapter Eight: Fears

Cleaning their old home the next week, Mid felt as if she were working twelve-hour days in a nineteenth-century sweatshop. Washing floors and walls, she found out the boys had been right about how little the exhaust fan cooled the second floor. It reminded her of the time she visited a college friend in New Orleans in the middle of an August heat wave.

Every evening she staggered back across Fairfield to a second house in disarray. Most of the furniture was in the right place, but half-unpacked boxes all around made even the large rooms seem crowded. Cooking and eating utensils were out in the kitchen, but with the new dishwasher waiting installation, piles of dirty plates, pots, and silverware surrounded the sink. In the family room--something new for the Lindblooms--sofa and chairs were haphazardly arranged. Mid also felt her family members were no longer in the correct places.

To make matters worse, she had no fellow workers. Curtis was out of town on his job, and Oscar was gone mornings to teach and spent afternoons preparing his next class. Carol took as many shifts as she could get at the drugstore and began a twice-daily training program--with her unknown university student friend. She was scheduled for her Army physical in a month.

Scrubbing the insides of closets that had not been cleaned in decades, Mid thought about women who worked in factories during the Depression and earlier. She recalled specifically the Radium Girls of Orange, New Jersey. During the time of World War II, they were hired to cover military watch dials with paint that glowed in the dark; 250 dials a day could earn about $4.00. Encouraged to use their lips or tongues to keep the brushes pointed, a number contracted radiation poisoning. A handful of them sued, and their case, settled in 1928, received a lot of attention in the area where Mid grew up.

The house on Limestone had no radium (though, looking back years later, she would be aware that the asbestos shingles and insulation might have posed a health hazard). At the time, Mid, proud of her ability to work hard for long hours, never thought she would get ill.

At one point, though, she wondered if, in the past, she hadn't inadvertently contributed to current factors affecting women's health. At college, she had worked with a small group of physiology majors under the direction of a woman doctor. The physical capacities of women were measured scientifically, producing data that contradicted a weaker stereotype carried forward from the Victorian period. Their publications helped make the case that women were capable of strenuous work; but the new employment opportunities for women in factories during the war years made the women vulnerable to exploitation.

60

With her college education, Mid never had to consider undertaking such labor herself and was able, with her father's help, to get work as a medical technologist. But she knew about women who, with the men gone away to fight, took industrial jobs (Rosie the Riveter) where they were subject to workplace accidents and illnesses. Later, when peace came, they lost their positions; they were told to go home, take care of their returning husbands, raise children. Progress and regression in her own generation.

Now she had a daughter wanting to become a soldier. The only good thing about that was that it would probably end whatever relationship she had with this college student. General Westmoreland was allowing women to serve as nurses and clerks in this new war, but in a conflict without clear lines dividing friend from foe, could they know what roles they might have to play? The more fit Carol became, thought Mid, the more likely she could find herself in dangerous situations. She decided it was time to tell her daughter about Marilyn.

"She was from California," Mid explained one evening. "And I thought of her as my West Coast twin when we met as Red Cross volunteers."

"Did you look alike?"

"Yes, same size and shape, though her hair was lighter. But we got along from the first, especially after we were thought to be prostitutes."

"Prostitutes?"

"On the Continent, I learned, 'camp followers'--whores--wore pants and the same uniforms as the men. So, when some of the French soldiers saw us in our outfits, they assumed our — 'services' — involved more than providing donuts."

"Ah, it seemed like you'd gone back to the world's oldest profession. And I thought you were crossing frontiers as a New Woman."

Mid and Carol were on the patio in the back of the new house; there was a nice breeze and the temperature had dropped a few degrees after a thundershower. They could see each other reflected in the double glass doors of the family room. As night came on, Oscar would become visible through the glass in his recliner, smoking his pipe and watching television.

"I did believe we Red Cross girls were breaking new ground. I became a truck driver."

"You were in supply?"

"In a way. I drove a 'Clubmobile,' a truck with a donut-making machine. We'd go where the troops were, make a few thousand donuts, hand them out, and try to encourage the boys before they went into battle. Marilyn and I were really good at it, and we became close--closer even than sisters."

As she talked, Mid wondered how honest to be in telling this story. The job was physically demanding--driving and repairing trucks, hauling huge bags of flour, kneading pounds of dough--and at times dangerous. The oil in the machine had to be kept very hot, and few of the girls escaped burns from spills and leaks. But those were minor worries during the Blitz.

At the same time, they were exhilarated at the opportunity to take on tasks generally reserved for men. They were given the informal military rank of captain and a carefully designed uniform to reinforce an authority unique to their environment. And once the Clubmobile took off on a run, they were completely in charge.

"You were in England or on the Continent?"

"Red Cross volunteers went all over--Africa, India, the Pacific. They were desperate to get help, so, rather than a six-week training course, I only had to do two weeks."

"I read that there was a lot of emphasis on 'feminine' behavior, making sure the men respected you and behaved properly."

"You know, that was never a problem. At least with the enlisted men."

She recalls how Marilyn had slipped a raincoat over nothing one evening to carry a bucket of hot water from the mess hall for a bath. After she told Mid a sergeant had politely told her she might want to wear something warmer the next time she went out, they discovered a tear in her coat, which had exposed her backside. But no one later referred to the incident.

"Officers were a problem?"

"We were not supposed to have relationships with enlisted men, and sometimes the officers thought that meant we should be willing to be entertained by them—or the other way around. But most understood the code." She took a sip of her iced tea. "I'm not sure it's the same today, with all the changes in sexual mores."

Carol didn't take the bait, so Mid decided she'd better go on. "What we didn't anticipate, though, was the way the men wanted us to ease their fears going into battle. Oh, they'd talk as if they were ready to take on Jerry and laugh at the danger with each other. But with us—with some of us, especially—they were just little boys who wanted to be back with their mothers."

"I guess a lot of them were young," mused Carol.

"Well, even some of the older ones, if they were alone with you, they'd confess."

"That must have been hard."

Mid breathed deeply. "The worst for me was a group on a train that had to stop to let another train pass on its way to hospital with wounded soldiers. We heard them, too."

"Heard them?"

"Many had been burned and were in horrible pain. A ship had been torpedoed, I think, and those that didn't jump into the water right away—So, anyway, when the train with the injured soldiers went on, we tried to ease the fears of the other boys."

Mid had been burned numerous times by the donut cooking oil and knew how much those minor injuries hurt and how long they took to heal. The wounded soldiers had second and third degree burns all over their bodies, some had been blinded, many would suffer days before dying. It had been worse than she'd ever imagined about sinners engulfed in the fires of hell.

"Mom, I'll never be on a train like that."

"Good." Mid thought she wasn't going to have to tell her that Marilyn had never recovered from the encounter with the burned soldiers.

"If I'm going to die young, it will be on the battlefield, not being carried away from it."

# Chapter Nine: Measures

"Before you go out," Mid said to Curtis Friday afternoon, "tell us about well-finding." He had returned from the West Plains area at noon and finished up his paperwork at the office. He was only stopping at the house long enough to change clothes, grab a bite to eat, and head off to Newtown. Having already let Carol slip away--another training run with her student friend--Mid wanted to exert some control in the family.

"Actually, I found it slower going than I'd thought." Curtis was looking in the refrigerator for leftovers. The kitchen had a wide pass-through to the family room, so his parents could hear and see him without getting up. They would not have dinner themselves for another hour.

"How so?" his father asked from his recliner. He cut back the volume on the new television, one of the things he had insisted on as part of the move.

"Well, you know I have to set an altimeter so I can get an accurate reading of the elevation at the well site. But altimeters drift as the weather changes--rising air pressure, or falling--and I need to be back at a location with known elevation inside of an hour in order to calculate the drift over time and adjust the reading."

"So if you don't, you have to do it all over again--set the altimeter, go to the site, return to the original or another place with a known elevation?"

"Exactly. In that case, I'm back at square one, but 90 minutes have passed. I feel like it's all *déjà vu*." He had put some Jell-O salad, cold meatloaf, and bread on the pass-through counter and come around to make a meal at the dinette. "So, there were, ah, a few setbacks."

Satisfied, Oscar eased the television volume back up to hear the news. He had positioned his favorite recliner by the double patio doors so that he had a view of their spacious backyard to his right during the day; and yet, because of the awning over the patio, there was no glare on the new television during the afternoon. If cars were an early indulgence of Oscar's professional success, this mahogany console Zenith with round-screen color was a later one.

The Jaguar sedan, being British, linked him to the tradition of European aristocracy; but as an oddity for a Midwestern small town, his car was also connected to new and sometimes startling innovation ahead. When gas prices skyrocketed in the 1970s, economical foreign cars would become commonplace even in small towns.

The Zenith television was similar: on the one hand, it retained the hand-wiring of older models when other brands were switching to mass-manufactured circuit boards as production shortcuts; on the other hand, including the latest in refinement of remote control and advanced color channel tuning, it represented cutting-edge technology. Oscar remained an odd combination of conservative and innovative impulses.

Sitting at the dinette across from Curtis, Mid switched the subject to what she was interested in. "Now you're off to help at the Turntable. Does your--um, friend--work there full-time?"

"Sarah. More than full-time. She's a waitress, hostess, dishwasher, table setter--you name it. Like me, she's saving for the future."

"College?"

"Art school. Later she wants to have her own studio."

"As a painter, photographer, sculptor?"

"All of the above. And she wants to design buildings."

"Ambitious!"

"She has reason to be. She's a prodigy, been winning awards for creativity since she was ten. Because her father's been all over--he's in the Army--she's studied in Europe, Asia, Japan."

"My goodness! He must be talented, too."

"I guess so, but her mother's her inspiration. She's a direct descendent of Queen Emma."

"I don't remember a British monarch named Emma."

"Oh, Emma was Hawaiian, though she became a friend of Queen Victoria. Sarah also traces her family lines to China, Italy, Africa, as well as Hawaii. She's a bit of an oddity in staid little Fairfield."

Mid thought how she herself was descended from one of the Lacys who came to this country on the Mayflower. She was as American as she could be. Oscar's father was Swedish, but he'd grown up without learning any of that language and little of Scandinavia's traditions. So their own children were raised in this country's heartland, essential W.A.S.P.s (though the Protestant element was decidedly muted).

"I can see how such a girl would seem exotic. Does she look — foreign?"

"Some people thinks she's Oriental; some even wonder if she's Afro-American. She won't say what she is. Claims it doesn't matter."

Blacks in Fairfield used to have to go all the way to Jefferson City, an hour away, for high school. There had been a separate ("Negro") elementary school as well, with so small a population that a single teacher was responsible for all grades. Although all schools were integrated in 1954, there had been no interracial dating among Curtis' set--as least as far as Mid knew. Had there been, she felt sure she would have heard about it from other parents.

Mid was sure she had no prejudices herself, but she believed it would be hard for a mixed couple confronting the biases of others. And children of interracial couples! They would have no place in either white or black culture.

*"What am I doing?"* she thought. *"I'm racing way ahead of myself in these thoughts. After all, he said they were just friends. At the worst there might be some flirtation, maybe—maybe even some sort of summer romance he'll look back on years later, probably with the appropriate embarrassment— Or maybe I will!"*

"Thanks for the grub, Mom," Curtis said and set his plate up on the counter. Stepping quickly around to the other side, he slid them into the dishwater. Across the pass-through, he grinned. "I'll be back by a reasonable time. It's off to recount my well-finding adventures to another audience."

As he hurried toward the front door, patting his mother on a shoulder, he sang a phrase from a popular song--*"ticket to ri-ide."* She would learn of the risqué meaning of those Beatles lyrics many years later; but she today noticed only that his eyes were bright and his step lively.

The image of his smiling face brought back a memory of the look his father had presented through an office door the year they met. Oscar was, it would turn out, about to ask her to go to the movies, their first date. She saw him through the glass grinning excitedly and holding up two cups he had carried from the cafeteria. Like most in the office, they drank black coffee all day long.

Oscar was whistling the tune to "Coming in on a Wing and a Prayer," a popular war song. The words of that hit are sung by the crew of a bomber returning from a mission with one motor out and a radio operator scanning the skies for missing aircraft. Mid hadn't wanted to hear the words back then.

70

They were both working at the Health Department in Jefferson City, she in the lab and he doing studies of data they produced and material from other labs across the country. Taking this job had been for Mid a way of forgetting what had happened to Marilyn (and others), as well as a determined step forward in her life. If true love hadn't found her in the East, she'd look for it in another place. And just in case she would never marry, she viewed this job in a different part of the country as a turning point in her career.

Oscar didn't have particular reasons to visit Mid in the lab but was creative in concocting them. One day he stepped in from the hall insisting he had heard microbes talking from her slides ("One just asked another, 'you really think you need glasses at your age?'"). He also sought Mid out in the cafeteria, telling her about a fictional office worker ("Al Laddin") he had made up who appeared and disappeared from routine reports. And for a week he walked backwards wherever he needed to go, "just to see what it's like," more than once backing into the lab as if he'd gotten confused about where he was.

He was silly but very good at his work. He got along with men in the office, though it didn't seem that he spent time with them away from work. And there was a sadness beneath his antics, a suggestion that he had great dreams, which had been put on hold for others.

In the words of Harold Adamson and Jimmie McHugh in the hit war song, this boy was "coming in" to Mid's lab "on a prayer," though without "faith in the

Lord." Mid realized she would have to answer his need. And that she wanted to. But what did sophisticated and worldly Sarah Bridges think of a boy as eager and as innocent as his father had been a generation earlier?

# Chapter Ten: Times

"Do you know a student named Aaron?" Mid asked Oscar. "I think he's in one of your summer courses." She was unpacking the Lacy mantel clock on the dinette in the family room, careful to keep it level.

"Looking for tall, dark, and handsome?"

"He's the one Carol's been seeing. He could be behind her sudden interest in the military."

While her clock needed an overhaul, Mid had decided to set it up on the cherry sideboard for now. There were many other things to take care of before she could find a new repairman; but she could clean up the marble case with a mild detergent and polish the surface. It would be comforting to see it in place, though it would be even more reassuring when the chimes rang on the half hour and the hour. Those were sounds she'd heard growing up in Rutherford, New Jersey; she wanted to continue enjoying their echoes, as it were, in Fairfield.

"I hope he's not one of our foreign students," said Oscar. He often complained that the university was giving future scientists and engineers from other countries the best of American knowledge. They would use their learning to build up their own nations, he said, undermining American strength in the world. In the Cold War, if you weren't alert, you would find yourself on the downward path of all empires.

"As far as I know, he's a red-blooded citizen of the United States. I was just wondering how old he was, if he was—you know, taking advantage of a young and idealistic girl, uncertain about which way to turn at this crucial point in her life."

Mid unwrapped the clock pendulum bob and the rod by which it attached to the works. She would keep them in a drawer of the sideboard for now. As she inspected the parts, a wishful thought came to her that traveling across town in the trunk of the Rambler might have healed this antique of its woes. If she put it in place now, perhaps she'd merely have to level the case and set the beat, following the procedure she'd watched Mr. Agee use several times.

"Carol's pretty steady, like you were." Oscar's praise of Mid was sometimes a compliment to himself as the man who had won her. "I think she sees her summer as uneventful and is talking about enlisting just to give herself some drama. She'll be in Columbia come September."

"We've been lucky with our children," mused Mid. "In other parts of the country, young people are acting crazy--getting involved in boycotts, sit-ins, all sorts of things. The Midwest is a calm between the storms of East and West Coast."

"Well, anyway. You know I learn students by their last names. I'll have to take a look at the roll and see if there are any suspects. That reminds me, Sarge:

there's a reception of sorts at the new humanities center next weekend. Would you like to go for an hour or so?"

Mid looked at him, half-reclined in his favorite chair. "You never want to go to those things. What's the occasion?"

"Oh, stirring up interest in the new drama program. Miss—Professor Baudin made a special point of asking me, and since I've agreed to help with *Come Back, Little Sheba*—"

Mid tried to curb her irritation. She'd accepted her husband's devotion to the nuclear family so completely that her friends knew not even to invite her to this kind of activity. The two physics department picnics, when he sometimes had a chance to play softball, were his major social events of the year. Watching him turn pages in *Car and Driver* now without looking up confirmed that he knew this was not like him.

"Who else will be coming? Is it a university wide event?"

"One of your admirers, apparently--Arthur James."

"He admires all women. He hardly speaks to me."

"Hmm. He told me this week I was fortunate to be married to such an attractive lady."

"You should suggest he spend time with the new theater teacher rather than married women. I assume she's single."

"Divorced, I think; no children. And I don't believe she's interested in marrying again."

"We'd better devote the weekend to getting over the hump of putting things away."

Mid was finding it hard not to fuss about how Oscar sat in his chair. He had a habit of stopping in the mid-point of reclining, neither sitting upright nor reclining, almost like tipping a straight-back chair on its legs. *Come in or go out,* she thought; *Go in or come out.* Years later, when another generation of recliners came along, she found Oscar's variable stopping point had anticipated more sophisticated chairs of the future

Oscar glanced around the room. "Hmm. I thought we had the back of it broken?"

"I think it's my back that's broken." She picked up the clock and headed toward the living room. Whether that was the exact moment she envisioned a special place for herself in this new house, or whether that inspiration came shortly before or after, Mid couldn't say. Nevertheless, she recorded this event as the turning point in her movement toward living in an empty nest with a middle-aged husband who was finding new interests on his own.

All their possessions were now out of the house on Limestone Drive, and the new owner was coming Monday for a final inspection. The clutter in every room of their new home, however, threatened to occupy Mid for the rest of the summer. Why not see that process as more than the realization of an easier living situation for the two of them? It should also be a fresh start for herself alone.

Mid realized she needed her own space to represent freedom from the household demands that had governed her life for a quarter of a century; but she also wanted a location for the cultivation of a new avocation, even if it would take her until the fall to begin it.

Over the last few years, the children grown, she had found domestic chores taking less and less of her time. Especially in this community dominated by science, people took advantage of labor-saving devices, from washing machines and dishwashers to frozen foods and TV dinners. New materials in home building, like no-wax vinyl floors, made housekeeping easier; and a general prosperity gave women the opportunity to enjoy hobbies, return to school, take jobs. Mid realized she had whole days ahead without major chores: what should she do?

She wandered out to the utility room behind the garage, a spacious, heated space off the kitchen. When they had first looked at the house, she saw it as the place for laundry, sewing, and puttering. On Limestone, her washer had been in the kitchen, and she had to hang clothes outside in the summer, in the basement over the winter. She'd planned to use moveable metal clothes racks and folding wooden drying racks here. Since one end of the utility room faced south, she might build shelves to hold plants by the windows.

But now, she thought, this could also become an office, too. It wouldn't restrict the laundry operation-- after all, there were just the two of them! The sewing machine fit neatly to one side of the door from the

77

kitchen; and she had an old floor lamp (not needed elsewhere in this more modern home) to provide illumination. She could set up another work space in front of the windows on the west side of the room, perhaps adding a nice area rug and her own recliner.

Looking at this scene, an avocation seemed to spring full blown into her consciousness. Starting with the Lacy family heirloom, she would service old mantel, wall, and cuckoo clocks. After all, such a hobby did not take a lot of space, unless you worked on grandfather clocks. (Timepieces associated with men did not appeal to her at this moment!)

Always good with her hands, she used her father-in-law's carpentry tools, some brought all the way from Sweden, more than Oscar did. While he was good at imagining and drawing mechanical constructions, even writing formulas to show why his proportions and sizes were correct, he left the task of completion to others. For Mid, this was leaving the project suspended in the middle--initiated but not completed.

Then a further thought came to Mid. Not only would this be a hobby, but she would create a bona fide business. After all, Mr. Agee's retirement had created a vacuum that no else locally seemed eager to fill. The basic tools would not be expensive, and Grandpa's old desk, with its many cubbyholes, would serve nicely to hold tools and parts.

Of course, it would probably be hard to turn a profit in such a venture. In this age, people wanted modern battery-driven timepieces. Self-winding wristwatches and electric clocks were commonplace. (She couldn't know it, of course, but quartz watches would come in just a few years, revolutionizing the industry even more). People tended to put their old mechanical clocks in the attic rather than undertake the expense of having them cleaned and adjusted regularly. But once people knew there was someone who might restore them for an economical fee, —

Today, then, she staked her claim on this space for an office/workroom--"Utility-ization." And, when a few more things were in place, she would become — um — Mrs. Clockwork. . . or Miss Time — or the Now Girl.

# Volume Two: Stream

# Chapter Eleven: Codes

"Suppose for a moment that you are a prisoner of war," began Aaron.

"I don't want to do that," Mid responded.

"It's just hypothetical, Mom," reassured Carol, "to show how cryptology works."

Images of the Bataan Death March and German concentration camps had sprung up in Mid's mind so quickly that she balked at even a hypothetical consideration of prisoners of war. Her generation was haunted by newsreel images of emaciated human figures discovered by Allied troops. They wanted somehow to go back into time and prevent what had happened. Now they were reading that pilots were being shot down over North Vietnam and taken prisoner.

Mid offered, "You could use a different situation. Say, a husband and wife who have to communicate without any of their children understanding what they're up to."

"What *are* they up to?" asked Oscar, muting the television with his remote. Mid wondered how he had heard when most of the time he seemed lost in whatever show he was watching--or in his own dreams.

"Oh, the usual--a romantic getaway to rekindle their romance. But they can't let the children know how badly they need it. Not the seven-year-itch, but maybe the 25-year blues."

"Ah," said Oscar and returned to watching television

Carol studied her mother. "Okay. A bit strange for using code, but go ahead, Aaron."

"Right. So, let's see—before they sit down to dinner in the evening--with how many children?" On his second visit to the Lindblooms' home, it was clear he was a bit nervous.

"Three," said Mid. "Two boys and a girl, wonderful, nearly grown young people."

She was tolerating her daughter's "friend" tonight, though she had hoped to have only her family for the Fourth of July weekend. Her goal had been to get them to arrange things in the guest bedrooms--the two boys taking the front room, Carol the one at the end of the hall by her parents. Unpacked boxes were in both. Between the two was Oscar's study, already organized.

Carol had launched into her explanation of code while helping Mid prepare dinner for family members and guests. It would be the largest gathering in either of the Lindblooms' Fairfield houses, though tomorrow's was to be even larger. Mid was sure Oscar would spend a lot of the weekend in his study.

"All right, then," Aaron continued. "That morning they had each taken identical pads of paper. The pages on both pads have the same random sequences of numbers. No two pages in one pad are the same, but the two pads have the exact same pages in the same order."

"Ah," Mid said. "So, each number on a given page corresponds to a letter?"

"Right. The first number on the grid is A, the second B, etc., though the system can be made more complicated by modular arithmetic. Still, all the person writing in code, or the one reading, has to do is substitute the appropriate letter for the number. So, one person--let's say the mother, in the kitchen preparing dinner—"

"Of course," Mid muttered, peeling potatoes at the sink while Carol and Aaron sat at the dinette.

"—the one preparing dinner uses the grid on the fifth page to encode a message on a blank piece of paper. The twenty-fifth number on the page, whatever it is, stands for the twenty-fifth letter of the alphabet--'Y'."

*"Why" indeed*, Mid thought to herself.

Carol continued. "She completes her message one number/letter at a time and slips it into her husband's dinner roll."

"And," finished Aaron, "without letting the children--wonderful though they are--see, he slips the paper into his pocket to decode later."

"In his study later," Oscar added from his recliner, "he decodes the message by replacing the numbers on his sheet with the correct letters: --'*You are still the man of my dreams*'."

Mid frowned. "Of course, he then eats the piece of paper--the dinner wasn't exactly to his satisfaction--and goes to bed early."

Carol exchanged glances with Aaron and concluded, "Well, the point of all this is to say cryptographers are coming up with ways to generate those random number sequences more quickly by using machines, kind of advanced calculators."

"And that's why your daughter would be such an asset to the military. With her math skills, she can cut a good deal and get excellent training for the future. The world is a'changing."

Mid had concluded weeks ago that arguing with Carol about her new plan to delay college and get experience in the military would not be productive. Her daughter was too strong willed, and, like others in her generation, would not accept the values her parents had held when they were young.

Aaron, it turned out, had served three years in the Army right out of high school and was now using the GI Bill to study electrical engineering at SCMSU. Mid wanted to ask him, if being a soldier would be so good for Carol, why hadn't he stayed in?

She wondered if it had anything to do with his race. Aaron's father had married a Japanese woman. Though his speech was as American as Carol's, his looks favored his mother. Many of Mid's friends could not move past their hatred of "the Japs" and were automatically suspicious of anyone who looked Oriental. This anger might be even worse among soldiers.

Mid turned to check on the meatloaf in the oven. "She still needs to get things down in black and white. I've read about how new recruits later find themselves in situations they didn't sign up for. Then it's too late to go back to their civilian lives."

After a pause, Carol asked, "Are we going to the fireworks this year?" It was clear she was ready to change the subject.

"I think we can see them down by that turnaround," offered Oscar. There's a gap through the trees there, and the Lions Club grounds are just over a slight ridge."

Mid agreed, knowing he would resist joining the crowd that traditionally came to picnic and celebrate along the shore of the Lions Club's little lake. His weekend already had him entangled in more social situations than he liked.

She was almost tempted to stay home herself and knit or work on her clock. Curtis was bringing Sarah from Newtown soon--another cause for anxiety. And Louis had surprised them by asking if "a friend" could travel with him from St. Louis tomorrow. Who would that be?

Things had certainly diverged from the trajectories she had foreseen when she and Oscar signed the papers for the new house back in April. Her interpretation of the signs then must have depended on a bad code. She had one set of random number pages, everyone in her family different ones. And sadly, perhaps she had misread Oscar the most.

Ever since that first social occasion promoting the new theater program, she had been troubled by his behavior. He acted like a schoolboy sometimes, alternately exuberant and then vaguely depressed. And more than once he was simply mean.

On that earlier occasion Arthur James had been entertaining a small group of the theater students (who, of course, liked a show). "I'm going to put this ping-pong ball in this cup" he said, holding up the two white objects. "And then the ball will disappear." He dropped the ball, waved his hand over the cup, turned it upside down, shook it, waved it. "Empty!" he declared.

Mid was chatting with some of the members of her bridge group by the punch table and looked over to see Arthur wink conspiratorially at her. She also noted that Professor Baudin had joined the group.

"It's like a lady's love," James continued in vaudeville banter, his gaze fixed on Mid. "Now you have it, now you don't." Then he asked a pretty redhead, "Where is it hiding?"

She crossed her arms across her chest, as if worried the ball would reappear there. "Got me."

"I wish I did," Arthur grinned. "Maybe the ball— is. . . in my—pocket."

He set the cup down and dug around in both pants pockets. "Hmm. One in each." He pulled out two orange ping-pong balls. "But that's not the one that's missing." He looked around, then picked up the cup again. "Ah! I think it's reappeared." He slapped the cup upside down on the table, and the white ball rolled out.

"How did you do that?" asked the redheaded student.

"Just back up an hour or so in time," said Oscar, "and you'll see that Professor James brought a special cup and ball with him from his office. The ball sticks in the cup. But because it's the same color as the cup, it seems to have disappeared. It's been in there all along, pretending to be the bottom of the cup."

Mid could see Arthur's face fall.

# Chapter Twelve: Strikes

"What's all this?" Sarah asked. Curtis' guest was surveying the parts of the Lacy clock spread out on Mid's desktop in her "utility room/sewing room/office." She had arrived in time to have dinner and then helped clear the table; but Carol wouldn't let the guest do the dishes. The men were watching *Jonny Quest* in the family room.

Pointing to the marble case, which she'd set on the floor in the corner, Mid explained, "It's an old family clock. I couldn't find anyone to service it now that Mr. Agee at the jewelry store has retired, so I decided I'd take the project on myself--a new hobby."

"What a nice idea! I've always loved mechanical clocks, especially cuckoo clocks. You don't happen to have one of those?"

"No. Actually, this is my first effort, sort of a trial run. And if I can't make some progress pretty soon, I may have to give up on the idea."

Once she figured out how to take the hands off the face, Mid had had no trouble getting the works out of the case. There was a tiny nut holding them on that had gotten stuck over the years. She had put sewing machine oil on it, let that sit overnight, then worked it off carefully. The clock had been stopped at nine o'clock one day in the spring; and Mid wondered how many hours would pass unrecorded before it could reclaim its *raison d'être*.

Sarah said, "Cuckoos, the birds, are associated with spring. I think that's why I like the clocks, announcing a fresh start every hour."

Mid smiled inwardly at this optimistic view. "Of course," she pointed out, "the birds themselves are not so admirable--laying their eggs in the nests of other birds and letting them raise their young."

"True. There are also a number of unpleasant myths associated with them. Zeus seduced Hera by appearing as a beat up, rain-soaked cuckoo. When she held him to her breast, he reverted to his true form and raped her. She had to marry him to save her reputation."

"That's a cautionary tale, to be sure." Mid studied the clock's count wheel, which governed the times the hammer struck the chimes. She couldn't see how it fit in with the chain of gears that would raise and release the hammer.

"Do you have a book for clock repair?" Sarah asked. "I can't see going in there without some reference work to guide you."

Again Mid pointed, this time to a stack of books on the temporary brick and board shelves she'd put up on the other side of the door out to the patio. "Dr. Lindbloom found most of these for me at the university library. Apparently there was a faculty member some years ago who used clocks to teach mechanical engineering. And he stocked the library."

"Hmm. Someone being nostalgic or perhaps looking ahead to the day there will be a fad for old-fashioned timepieces. Can you tell me what you're doing now?" Sarah came to the side of the desk and leaned over, scanning the gears, levers, springs, and arbors.

Without turning toward her, Mid was aware of the deep gap in her blouse and the fullness of what was inside. This was a well-endowed girl!

She sighed. "To tell you the truth, I've cleaned all these parts and made a diagram of how they fit together, but I'm baffled how to get everything in place on the back plate and then attach the front plate--well, or the other way around. Nothing stays where it's supposed to."

She wasn't going to tell Sarah that she'd gotten impatient and disassembled the clock too quickly. She should have studied longer at each step, taken more detailed notes, and drawn better diagrams. She had vowed to be more deliberate next time—if there were a next time. "Curtis tells me you're an artist. Will you go to some specialized school for that?"

"Actually, I want to be an architect. I've done sculpture, watercolors, pen and ink drawings; and I'll take mechanical drawing this fall. But I want to see these representations take shape in three-dimensional reality. And before I try for architectural school, I want four years of study at a good liberal arts school."

"Ah, I'm afraid Fairfield wouldn't be the place for that. It's mostly engineers here."

"My parents think I should go to one of the Ivy League schools."

Mid looked up at the girl she had earlier assumed might aspire to become a beautician. "You're not interested in — um, settling down, having a family?"

Although Mid couldn't be sure--in part, because Sarah's skin was almost coffee-colored--she thought the girl blushed before saying, "Well, not immediately. There are so many things I need to do first. And, right now, I need Curtis to take me home, if I can tear him away from television. You've been so nice to include me in this weekend."

She bent down and put an arm across Mid's shoulders, hugging her. Then she went back to the family room.

Mid studied her attractive figure in the bright sundress as she stepped from the room. Did this talented girl have high goals that would take her away from Fairfield and Curtis, or was she so captivating he might follow her wherever she went. Sometimes Curtis seemed as impressionable as the young star of *Jonny Quest*.

Mid had watched a few episodes of this animated science-fiction/adventure show but didn't like the fact that the 12-year-old hero had no mother to guide him. With his father and friend, Race Bannon, he ended up in dangerous situations and sometimes witnessed the darker side of humanity. (In fact, the show would become a target of parents' groups concerned about the effect of its violence on children.)

Oscar often criticized what he called the show's "pseudo-science," but Mid knew he admired the physical skills and intellectual power of Jonny's father. Apparently uninterested in women after losing his wife, Dr. Quest was always able to outsmart villains. He not only identified them as culprits but exposed their tricks, which sometimes masqueraded as scientific breakthroughs. Like most viewers, Oscar disliked Dr. Zin, the Oriental arch-villain whose laugh was almost inhuman.

One recurring woman character on the show, Jade (Race Bannon's old girlfriend), seemed to be detached from any official government organization but sometimes became involved in the Quests' adventures. Apparently, she could tell the true identity of a man by kissing him. And many men wanted to kiss her! (*Hera should have had Jade's gift,* thought Mid, *when she held Zeus in his cuckoo form!*) Tonight, staring at her disconnected clock parts, Mid wondered what powers Sarah had.

Her athletic stride resembled Carol's. And they both had clear professional goals. Their clothes--with undone blouse buttons and hip-hugging slacks-- showed a pride in their bodies, which Mid was coming to realize reflected an attitude. Did they care about their figures for their own sake, not as ways to attract men? Such an attitude was foreign to Mid's generation.

Well, or was it? In college she had worked with female faculty to study the strength and endurance of women, helping to produce data that counteracted nineteenth-century stereotypes. The girls she had helped train took pride in their abilities just as many women would when they began to work in factories during the war. She thought of Rosie the Riveter's muscular arm on recruitment posters.

Mid had shared their pleasure at proving capable, but more in her learning than in her physical activity. She had always been attractive to men and simply followed conventional styles of dress without studying their effect. The fact that she had suitors-- though for many years not ones she found up to her own standards--reinforced a basic self-confidence.

Once she married, there was even less reason to follow fashion trends. She was a mother, a housekeeper, and occasionally (but only occasionally) her husband's companion at social events. She did go to regular meetings of the faculty wives (The Birds Club); but their numbers were dwindling as younger women had other interests and there were now at least a handful of female faculty. She played bridge with the Birds' bridge club, but for those occasions a simple housedress or skirt and blouse were sufficient.

As she and Oscar entered this new period of their lives, did she need to take specific steps to appear more desirable in his eyes? Did she have to enter a game she'd played effortlessly when young, but which now would require time, money, commitment? Recalling his appreciation of Eve Poole and other

Hollywood stars, perhaps she should. And there was, after all, Marsha Baudin.

"That was Louis on the phone, Mom," Carol called from the kitchen. "He and Suzanne will be here before lunch tomorrow." She had drawn out the word, *Suzanne*. Louis didn't have girlfriends. "Don't you think it's a bit sudden, him bringing someone home to meet the parents?"

"Ah, his friend is a girl! I didn't expect that." Mid sighed. "Well, if you ask me, all sorts of things are happening too early with you kids. And maybe too late for me."

# Chapter Thirteen: Settings

"You know, Mom," Curtis pointed out the next afternoon, "this may be the largest group you've entertained for dinner. About the only guest we had when we were kids was Dr. Rust. And he wasn't a particularly lively dinner companion."

He was right. They had Sunday dinners at Oscar's parents in Jefferson City every few weeks, but Sallie and Carl seldom came to Fairfield. Mid's family rarely traveled to the Midwest.

"Your dad wanted Dr. Rust to come for dinner. He felt sorry for him because he lived alone in a rented room those first years." Rust joined the department in the late 1950s, having just turned thirty and with a fiancée back in Cincinnati. She didn't tell Curtis that Bill Rust wasn't quite as dull as he seemed; but she herself hadn't learned about his private interests until recently.

Curtis was watching Mid slice peppers and carrots for her pot roast gravy. "Yeah, all they would talk about was physics--universal field theory or time travel or things we couldn't even begin to understand."

"Shop talk. But that is what they most have in common."

"Dr. Rust wasn't old," Curtis observed, "but he sure acted like he belonged in the past. Refusing to marry until he could afford to build a house and have children!"

Mid smiled, remembering William's stoic attitude. "He refused to go into debt, even with a mortgage. I think his parents were ruined in the Depression, and he lived economically, saving for the future. He and Linda are finally putting the second level on their house."

When he could afford the basement, which was finished as living space, William went back to Ohio, married, and brought his new bride to live in the first stage of their modest home. It was ten years before they completed the first story, converting the ground floor to guest, utility, and work rooms. Oscar and Mid had to admire the Rusts' adherence to principle, having married themselves with far less caution about the future.

"Anyway," Curtis went on, "we had to rearrange the dining room to fit five people in that small space. And now you're ready to entertain—how many will it be--eight? Wow. I hope Dad survives it."

Mid smiled at the way he said "we" had to arrange, as she'd done it all herself. Even now, it did not occur to him to help get ready for this meal. Carol might have, but she was out on a training run with Aaron. Louis had not arrived, and their father had closed himself off in his study early in the afternoon. It would never occur to him he could lend a hand in the kitchen.

Mid accepted some of the responsibility for the fact that Oscar's household chores were minimal even as he dictated what must be done. She knew his mother had established the pattern for her gifted son. Then, the intensities of graduate school and being a junior professor had reinforced the idea that he needed to be shielded from distractions. So while other families might plan Fourth of July picnics (cold cuts and salad) or backyard cook-outs (hot dogs and hamburgers), Oscar saw no reason to battle ants, mosquitoes, or flies. They would all sit at the table.

For this Independence Day weekend, though, Mid had insisted that, as it was the first real chance to take advantage of her new home, Oscar would take a bigger part in family activity. She could get him to put two of the six extra leafs in the dining room's old oak table.

On Limestone Drive, the massive table had been compressed into a circle; expanding it would have blocked passage from the kitchen to the living room or pressed someone up against a wall. Now Mid could seat eight comfortably, ten with a bit of maneuvering.

She had originally purchased the table on impulse, aware that it was too big for the house they were buying. An older couple in the department was retiring to Florida and wanted to scale back with the move. They offered the table at a price Mid couldn't pass up, and it resembled the one her family of siblings, parents, and grandparents had gathered around in Rutherford, N.J.

At that time there were a number of neighborhoods around Fairfield made up of modest two-bedroom houses built during and immediately after the war to accommodate expansion at nearby Fort Leonard Wood, the School of Mines, and the United States Geological Survey (which had its Midwestern headquarters here). She and Oscar found one they could afford in a neighborhood informally known as "The Circle" on the western edge of town.

Mid thought they'd be able to move up to a larger home once they were more established. And many of the families that had come to town about the same time they had later emigrated to new housing developments in the county. But it was all Mid could do to persuade Oscar to add two small bedrooms in their attic for the children. She couldn't convince him to turn the garage into a family room, as some had done, or to add on to the back of house. And her fine old table remained compressed into a space perhaps ten feet by ten feet.

During the years she was busy keeping house and raising children, she was able to repress her dissatisfaction. In Carol's last year at home, though, frustration had blossomed with a kind of urgency she didn't fully understand herself.

Today, thinking about what silver and plates to use at that table, it came to her: "It's grandchildren!" Of course, she wanted a place where her married children would come with their kids for holidays.

Her own parents had bought a small farm in rural New Jersey for their retirement, intending to expand the old house. When her father died suddenly, Ethel found a remarkably comfortable small cottage to host her children's families. In addition to the bedroom on the first floor, where she slept, there were three little rooms off a balcony above the large living room. Now Mid wanted a way to repeat that pattern of relatives coming together.

Opening the silver chest on the sideboard, she heard a bustle in the entryway and turned to receive a hug. "Hi, Mom. I want you to meet Suzanne, the new friend I've told you about."

"And you're the wonderful mother Lou has told me *so much* about!" said a slim, attractive brunette embracing her also. "Let me help with that."

Before Mid could object, Suzanne put her purse on a chair, took the silverware from her, and stepped back into the dining room. She moved so smoothly and quickly that, to Mid, it looked as if knives, forks, and spoons were magically appearing at eight places.

"These?" the girl asked, pointing to the china cabinet. When Mid nodded, dinner and bread plates lifted up on fingertips and arranged themselves around the table. There was a stack of napkins already on the table; but Suzanne took them off one at a time and, her hands almost a blur, folded them into swans that perched at each setting.

"This is going to be *sooo* nice!" Suzanne said, standing back and admiring the effect, her arms folded across her chest. "What do you need me to do in the kitchen?"

Mid couldn't think for a moment. "Oh, nothing—right now. Why don't you go in and visit with the others? I know Oscar wants to hear about your school, what you're studying."

"Oh, I don't think he wants to hear about home economics. And I'd rather stay and get to know you first, if that's all right. Lou can visit with the men. He tells me you sew and knit."

Louis shrugged as if his new friend was going to do whatever she wanted. But he smiled at the same time and went down the hall toward his father's study.

"Oh, my sewing is pretty ordinary, but there is a new baby sweater pattern I could show you." Mid looked at Suzanne's dress, a plain but pretty summer outfit. "You—did you make your dress? It's very nice."

"Thank you. Yes, I've made my own clothes ever so long. With four sisters and two brothers, we almost never had store bought things, even for our First Communion."

*First Communion*? Mid paused in the doorway to the utility room/sewing room/office, struck by a vision of her future, a vision she didn't want to see.

Her oldest son would have a large (Catholic) family, and his children would have dozens of (Catholic) cousins. The rest of the Lindbloom family, knowing how hard it would be for Louis and Suzanne to travel with a horde of offspring, came to visit them in the big city at the mansion earned by his lucrative law practice. Of course, Suzanne and her incredibly capable children would provide sumptuous feasts they would all talk about for days.

Curtis, living back east (or abroad!) with Sarah, would be working as a proofreader for her architectural firm; and they preferred to stay in the fine St. Louis luxury hotel she had designed--from which they could also attend important cultural events when in town--rather than her brother's home, let alone her mother-in-law's modest house in remote Fairfield. Carol, a career soldier, would never marry. Traveling from post to post in distant corners of the globe, she would only be able to arrange brief layovers near the St. Louis airport. To see her Oscar and Mid had to drive in from Fairfield.

"Today *is* a new beginning," Mid thought to herself. "But not the one I was hoping for."

# Chapter Fourteen: Poses

That evening, to Mid's surprise, Oscar was the model of the gregarious family man, joining in the dinner conversation and then, when they all moved into the family room, politely asking each of the guests about their interests. "Aaron," he asked, "Carol says you're a great trainer. Are you on the university track team?"

"I ran in high school, but now it's time for me to concentrate on grades."

"I've always liked the sprinters. Wasn't bad in my own day."

Carol eyed him. "You've never mentioned that, Dad."

Oscar was sitting in his recliner, but he had not tipped it back. The others were on the sofa and chairs pulled out from the dinette. "Oh, at Salinas Wesleyan, a small school, you could make almost any team. Now, Sarah, you look fit. Do you participate in a high school sport?"

"I play tennis, but they don't have a program at Fairfield."

"She's good," Curtis offered. "I watched her play against her father."

"He's the athlete in our family. He lets me use the doubles lines to make the match close. According to my mom, he thought about going pro before he got in the army."

"Well, Marian, we have some talented guests tonight. It's delightful to have them join us for this holiday meal."

Mid studied him, this jovial, engaged man, and decided to pursue the opportunity. "I've been telling you, Oscar, now that the children are on their own-- two of them at least--we should entertain more. But," turning toward the third guest, "we haven't asked Suzanne about sports."

Suzanne blushed but prettily. "Oh, I've never had the time, unfortunately. As the oldest in my family, I do a lot of cooking, cleaning, babysitting. I don't mind, of course. It's what I want to do—after college—just like my mom."

"Now, you don't want to settle down too soon," advised Oscar. "There's a lot out there women these days can do before they start having a family. Not the way it was in our day."

Mid raised her eyebrows. *In their day* she had worked for a number of years before marrying, living on her own and even traveling out of the country.

"Sometimes I think I went on too fast with my career," Oscar continued. "I got so absorbed in studying physics that I stopped doing a lot of the things I enjoyed. Well, and was good at. Did I ever tell you kids about writing scripts for radio shows when I was in college?"

Soon he was standing and recounting the plot of *The Proud Wife*, his spoof of a popular serial from the late 1930s, *The Scientist's Wife*. Oscar's heroine, Sissy Tine, used the first person plural to describe her husband's achievements, upstaging him at home and at social events.

Mid frowned, aware that she herself sometimes said things like "we got tenure" in such and such a year. Or she might refer to the time "we" came to join the faculty. She had done so because she believed Oscar liked to think of her as, in a sense, working for him as he worked for the university, not because she wanted to claim responsibility for his achievements.

"You know," Oscar observed, scanning the group around the room, "we have enough here to put on a little skit. That was something we did to develop our radio shows."

"Oh, I couldn't do that," objected Suzanne, putting a hand on Louis' arm. "I can't speak in public."

Carol said, "It might be fun. And we have time before the fireworks."

Curtis insisted, "The skit can be improvisational, where there's a basic situation, each of us has a distinctive personality, and then we just wing it."

Oscar agreed. "Good idea. Say, we can use the roles of *Come Back, Little Sheba*, a play I will be directing on campus next fall. I may update the plot a bit for the present day, of course."

"You're directing a play? When did this happen?" Carol asked. "You've never been interested in anything but physics and math."

He pointed a finger at her. "Just goes to show you don't know everything about your parents, young lady."

Mid thought: *I'm not sure I know everything about your parents!*

"So, let's see: Sarah you can be Marie, the star college athlete and the girlfriend of naive Bruce. Aaron, you're Turk, an artist who's asked her to model for a poster about sports."

Sarah raised her arms like the victor in a boxing match, while Aaron pulled a pen from his pocket, ready to draw on an imaginary sketchpad. Oscar added, "The two of you are just friends, but there could be some sparks between you. Louis, you be Doc, a reformed alcoholic."

Louis started to object. "Wait a minute. Me a drunk? Well, I guess, if I'm reformed—. But watch out," he winked at Suzanne. "I could revert to my evil ways at any moment."

"Right. Now, you and your wife, Lola, rent rooms to college students. So the scene will be Turk's room in Doc's house." He waved across the space between him and the entryway.

"Won't you need a mother for Turk?" asked Mid.

"Right--that's Lola. Carol, I guess you'll be mom. Try to look old and dumpy. That's how your husband,

Doc, sees you. You've had better days, of course, but that was years — *years* ago."

Louis laughed and pointed a finger at his sister. She shrugged and mussed up her hair.

Mid stared. "No part for me?"

"Hmm. You can be the prompter. If someone seems stumped, if the scene is dragging, you whisper suggestions, keep the show going. Of course, I'm the director. I'll call for the proper emotion, the gestures to go with the dialogue. So, let's see: Doc finds Marie in a provocative pose as Aaron draws. Wait, who's Bruce, Marie's trusting boyfriend? Ah, Curtis you can be the sweet and innocent guy."

"Typecasting," said Curtis. "So, Doc and I are going to come in on the modeling scene?"

"Yes, Doc first. He'll be upset, but also protective of Marie," agreed Oscar. "Too, his own long forgotten desires might surface when he sees a pretty girl looking especially pretty. Of course, this is improv, so we don't know for sure what will happen. All we can predict is that raw emotion will break out."

"I do keep my clothes on, though, right?" asked Sarah, smiling.

"Of course. You're pretty enough as is," said the animated, energetic Oscar. At that moment he reminded Mid of his younger self, clowning around when he was courting her at the health department in Jefferson City decades ago.

Oscar called for "Places, everyone," and then "Action!"

An angry Doc/Louis advanced from the entryway to find Marie/Sarah proudly facing him with her hands on her hips, her feet apart. She turned her head to look back over a shoulder at Turk/Aaron. "What's going on here?" asked Doc/Louis. She ignored him and pursed her lips toward Turk/Aaron. Mid's eyes widened.

Turk/Aaron looked shocked at the girl's pose, as if he hadn't realized how alluring Marie/Sarah could be. "Nuh . . .nuh—nothing!" he tells Doc/Louis. "She's a model. That's all. I was just making a poster to—to—"

Marie/Sarah's tongue wet her parted lips. Mid whispered, "*To raise awareness.*"

"To raise awareness of—of our school's athletic program."

"I don't think that's all that's rising here," said Lola/Carol angrily. "That girl was about to—about to make—" She raised her eyebrows, trying to remember names.

Mid reminded her, "*Turk.*"

"—to make *Turk* do something he shouldn't."

Oscar spoke from beside his recliner. "Now, Sarah, have fun with your part when Bruce comes in. You love him, but he can be unimaginative. And you enjoy flirting with other boys."

108

Sarah batted her eyes. "Why, Turk, you know you like looking at me--as a model, of course." She had spun around to face him, a hand resting on a hip cocked out to the side.

Bruce/Curtis stepped forward. "Hi, Sarah. I've just come to see if you're ready to go to church." He sees everyone else. "Oh, hello, Mr. and Mrs. —um— Doc. And hello, there, Turk. I haven't seen you see since you failed physics with that Professor Lightbulb. He's pretty tough. I guess that's why you're in summer school, to repeat that course."

Turk/Aaron shrugged. "I do have to raise my grades. And I also need to raise some dough. That's why I'm using my artistic talent to draw this pretty girl here for the college." He gazed at Marie/Sarah in a new way.

"Oh, Turk," smiled Marie/Sarah. "The way your eyes are feasting on me tells me so much more. But, that's okay. It's the Fourth of July, and we all get to show our independence."

# Chapter Fifteen: Fireworks

"Would you like to tell me what that was all about?" Mid asked, trying to mute her anger. They'd gone to their bedroom to get what they needed for walking to the turnaround and watching the fireworks.

"*That* was about nothing, except my going along with the program. Haven't you been after me to be more sociable, more like I was when we first met?"

"Well, yes, but you seemed *too* involved. And maybe too attentive to Sarah."

"Don't be silly. A director has to motivate the actors. Marie was the key to the whole scene. And it's just for this evening. Tomorrow everybody goes back to where they were--Louis and Suzanne, Sarah, Aaron. You and I return to — to our routine."

She pulled open the doors to her double closet. "You say that as if you're disappointed."

"Sometimes a change of pace can be good." He studied himself in the mirror over his dresser. "I'm always hearing that, in a marriage, you need to rekindle the excitement from time to time. And meeting new people can do that."

"I guess *I* need to get out more, then!"

"Once this house move is really over, there will be plenty of opportunities for you. Maybe painting landscapes or bird watching. I have to admit that the theater program has reminded me of what I could have been doing all these years. I wonder where my saxophone is?"

"Curtis put it in the study closet. It had been tucked away with your old college papers."

"Ah, that horn brings back memories! Did I ever tell you about playing with my crazy cousins that summer in Jefferson City? We were the Undertones."

"That was before you met me. And we agreed not to go back over those days, especially if there was romance involved. Did your group have a woman vocalist?"

They stepped out onto the front porch. The rest of the party had already started down the street. "No, no lead singer, though—Hey, we're going to be late. Did you get your old shirt?"

Mid held it up. To cover her arms against mosquitoes, who loved her, she wore one of his old shirts. Tonight, though, she thought it gave her a raggedy look. She watched Oscar go down the walk ahead of her with, it seemed to her, more lift in his step than she'd seen in ages. Sadly, she thought, bugs would probably be more likely tonight to put their lips on her (if they have lips!) than her husband.

It also occurred to her that her complete wardrobe, as it had existed on Limestone Drive, had reassembled here on Middlecourt. Everything hanging in that closet had been worn many times. Some outfits were at least twenty years old; none was new. Perhaps half she had made herself, and others had been passed down by friends.

This larger, modern house had been meant to express a new, more expansive lifestyle. With her guests here right now, at least this one weekend represented a change. But the individual self she presented to those new people was the same old mother and housewife she'd been.

In her other house, she'd had no full-length mirror, only the one on the back of her dresser and the one above the sink in the bathroom. When she'd really wanted a complete look at herself, she stood on the bed. Next weekend she would get Oscar to install a mirror on the back of her closet door. And she would make sure there was sufficient light to inspect her appearance.

On the walk to the creek, Louis fell back to walk beside her. Suzanne was ahead with Sarah on one side, Carol on the other; the other men made up a third group. "So, what do you think of her?" Mid's older son whispered, nodding.

"Suzanne? Oh, she's very nice. She certainly knows her way around a kitchen!"

"Just like you. And she's a serious student, making high grades. She could even finish college early if she didn't have to continue to help at home."

"What is *her* mother doing, if I might ask?"

"She's a nurse at—a St. Louis hospital. Irregular hours."

Mid suspected he had avoided saying a "Catholic" hospital. "And her father?"

"He's a train conductor on the Missouri-Pacific—that is, so long as passenger trains continue to run. He kind of belongs to an earlier era; but he's a good father and family man."

Mid didn't want to appear to be prying into the other family's affairs, so she asked, "What do you think about Carol going into the Army?"

"I don't like it much. I'm guessing her friend Aaron has encouraged the idea. She should go to Columbia and pursue her MRS-degree, if you ask me. The traditional ways are best."

"You may be right, but you'd be outvoted in this group. Sarah wants to be an architect, and your brother plans to study English but not teach. What's he going to do with himself, assuming he graduates?"

"Probably become a peacenik. I doubt if you have many of them around here, but I've seen pictures of anti-war protesters in the St. Louis papers. Curtis can write their speeches and send in op-ed columns to the newspapers. Serve him right if he got drafted."

"Oh, that won't happen. And he's still young, not as mature as you were at that age." She sighed. "Everyone is so open to new ideas these days."

Oscar dropped back behind Curtis and Aaron. Suzanne, looking over her shoulder, beckoned Louis forward. So, the parents found themselves side by side at the tail end of the procession.

They were passing the spot where the creek pooled and weeping willows had grown up around the banks. When they had been looking at houses in the neighborhood, Mid knew this would be her place of retreat, just as Crystal Pond had been on The Circle. She'd already gotten in the habit of walking down here in the middle of the morning, before it got too hot.

She was surprised she almost never met anyone else, especially as the town had put several nice benches in the shady areas. This was not officially a park, but the creek's path was protected by a town right of way.

"Have you heard about the Newtons?" Oscar asked. "She's asking for a divorce after twenty-seven years of marriage." Though they'd known them for years, the Newtons were now their neighbors on Middlecourt. He was on the faculty and Mid played bridge with Eleanor.

"I have. She's been unhappy for a long time. They don't do anything together, and Jack rides that Harley of his all over the country."

"'She should go with him. After all, he's provided for the family; she owes him that."

"Owes him? Don't you think raising those twins and keeping house all that time means he owes *her* something? And, remember, Ellie took care of his parents down in Springfield when their health began to fail."

"Still, a divorce? People just don't take that step after being together for such a long time." He brushed at some tiny bugs around his face. "Or do they?"

"Catherine left my poor brother Bill. Felt she'd given up everything to marry him without realizing he would find religion and take her to Gary, Indiana." The youngest Lacy child became the minister at a black church, putting strain on everyone in that family."Bill was too idealistic, harkening back to your Puritan ancestors and taking up causes."

"Well, what about Marvin, your friend in Salinas. After he bought that farm out in the country, Rose decided to move back into town and live with her mother."

"That was different. They never had children, and she insisted on keeping her job after the war. Poor Marv never had a regular home life."

"'Regular'? What does that mean? Does every wife have to stay home and have babies? For all you know, maybe they couldn't have children. There's no one model for a marriage."

"So, you think people don't marry for life anymore?"

"I didn't say that at all. It's just that each situation is different."

Ahead they could see the others stopped at the turnaround on top of a small rise. Fireworks appeared over the horizon, and the young people were ooh-ing and ah-ing. Sarah leaned into Curtis; Louis stood close to Suzanne. Oscar's calculations had been accurate: this was a fine place to view the fireworks without being deafened by the sound or crowded for space.

The crescendos of flash and boom that followed, however, were not the fireworks Mid remembered from that Fourth of July. It was Oscar saying, "I wonder if, considering how things are going between us, we shouldn't spend a little time apart, sort of like before we were married."

# Chapter Sixteen: Tickings

"I hear something ticking," said Curtis, poking his head in the doorway to the utility room. "Oh, my gosh! My mother, secret revolutionary, is a building a bomb!"

Mid looked up. "Ah, the jokester is home." Then she pointed to a little stand she'd built, attached to the end of her worktable with a C-clamp. "No explosives here. What you're hearing is the Lacy family clock in a partially restored condition." The mechanism from the clock was suspended on the stand, making the parts easier to see and adjust. The steady tick-tock, louder with the works outside the case, came from the escapement gear's rocking back and forth.

"But that's what bomb makers do--remove the innards of a clock, put the thing in a—a case that looks like, oh, a flower vase; but it's really packed with explosives. I bet you stole them from the Fourth of July fireworks show, didn't you? Talk about 'utility-ization!'"

Mid could have told him the bombshell that day had been emotional, not physical. And that she felt there was a clock marking off either her marriage's continuation or its slow demise.

"No. As I explained to your friend, Sarah, I took apart my clock, cleaned each piece thoroughly, and reassembled the works. Unfortunately, the chime parts aren't working together, though the time portion is running, if a bit slowly."

She didn't admit that there had been frustrating moments in the repair process. As she tried to fit one piece into a plate, another part would slip out of its bushing on the other plate. But she hoped such an operation would be easier the next time.

"Sure, I see it is working, but what are you going to send sky high, Mom?"

Curtis was home this Friday afternoon, having spent the week searching for wells in Ralls County, where the famous Mark Twain Cave is located. Mid knew he would be going to meet Sarah as soon as he spent a polite few hours with his parents.

Mid pointed to a cardboard box beside her worktable. "Whatever it is, I could use this other system, couldn't I?"

"A cuckoo clock! Neat. Sarah will want to see it. Where did you find it?"

"It's more that it found me. I told my bridge group about the idea of starting a clock repair business, and the next day Charlotte Miller brought it by. She said it had been sitting out in the barn for who knows how long, and I was welcome to see if I could bring it back to life."

"It sounds like you're having fun. Speaking of fun, I took the Mark Twain Cave tour one evening after work."

"I did that with the faculty wives group years ago. Your dad, as you know, isn't much on visiting tourist places."

"I'd like to take Sarah. I could be Tom Sawyer escorting Becky Thatcher on a tour of the boys' hideout."

"It's not that long before you have to be back at school." She was hoping he understood his time with Sarah was close to an end. He now spent almost every minute with her when he was back in town. And, despite herself, Mid couldn't help worrying that their relationship involved activities never described for Twain's Victorian audience.

"Yes, but that doesn't mean I won't see her again. You know I have to come home to check on you, especially with Carol gone. You'll need cheering up." He was reminding her of another of her worries: Carol had passed her Army physical and would be inducted in two weeks.

In the tiny clock world of arbors and wheels, springs and levers, escapement and pendulum, there were no emotional forces skewing the movement of parts. Once correctly configured and put in beat, the system would run smoothly so long as energy was added once a week by winding the spring. The tick-tock of its world was driven by a metal coil; but human hearts — oh, dear!--they drove us all haywire.

119

What was she worrying about, though, with Curtis and Sarah? Mid knew she'd let her vague ideas about the Sexual Revolution attach themselves to this girl because she had lived in California, dressed to show her physical beauty, and possessed a self-confidence that seemed to intimidate her son. That shouldn't mean that Sarah embraced the "free love" Mid read about in popular magazines.

Oscar had had "the talk" with both boys before they were even interested in girls. And, like a good father of these times, he'd stressed the ease with which a girl could get pregnant and the disastrous consequences for her (less severe, of course, for the boy because she was the one responsible for saying "no"). Once sexual intercourse occurred, Oscar insisted (aware that it wasn't true), the odds were high that impregnation, gestation, and birth followed in ruthlessly regular order.

She thought about the apparent ignorance of sex shared by Tom Sawyer and Huck Finn. Despite their acquaintance with danger and bad men, Samuel Clemens and his boyhood friends were no more tempted to immoral behavior with girls, Mid believed, than his fictional characters: they all lived in a fantasy world.

When she and others in the Bird Club followed the tour guide through Mark Twain's Cave, they were shown rooms named after heroes and heroines like Aladdin and Jesse James. The famous author and his friends visited the many passages of the cave, carrying candles for illumination and entertaining each other with ghost stories, adventure tales, and fantasies.

120

Mid recalled her childhood summers at the family campsite on Greenwood Lake in New Jersey. She and her siblings had been free to roam the woods, which also had caves (though smaller than the Show Me state's), and spin innocent yarns about romantic figures--the Three Musketeers, Joan of Arc, Richard the Lionhearted. What tales would Sarah tell Curtis if the two found their way to Bridal Cave up near Camdenton?

An Osage maiden, so that story went, escaped the man she was supposed to marry by leaping from a cliff hundreds of feet above a rushing river. The girl would die if she couldn't have the man she loved. But that narrative could be revised to feature a man who defied his family and ran off with a woman from another tribe.

Although Mid could envision Curtis falling victim to a more experienced woman, oddly it didn't occur to her that Carol might succumb to the charms of someone like Aaron. Was it because she, not Oscar, had been the one to have "the talk" with her? She had been emphatic about the necessity for women to anticipate and control masculine appetite. Too, she counted on Carol's fierce independence, her insistence that she would determine her own destiny.

When Carol had left to meet Aaron at the track that afternoon, Mid had been struck again by her daughter's beauty: her long legs (conspicuous in her short shorts), firm bosom (tight T-shirt), and overall energy (bright cheeks, big smile, clear eyes). Of course, boys would find her attractive! Some might even assume that her intense physical training meant she

121

would welcome contact with boys that went beyond appropriately restrained embraces and kisses.

Mid had carried over to the present a set of standards that had protected her and her sisters thirty years ago and innocently assumed Carol would accept them. Girls matured faster now though, she realized, and Carol looked every bit a woman. Men in the past were allowed to girl watch; but this age's males, even older men, wanted to do more.

Arthur James had made remarks to her that would never have been uttered thirty years ago. Did Mid herself have to be alert to new dangers? If she had been protected by class and nature as a young woman, how was she protected now? Oh my, she realized, by her age!

Mid remembered when had been climbing the ladder to the attic in the old house and her daughter told her to cover up her legs. Mentally, Mid now compared her body with her daughter's--soft where Carol was firm, stooped while her daughter stood straight, stiff when her child was flexible.

Despite her medical experience, Mid did not think beyond the terms used by her friends to talk about their aging--"change of life," "female trouble," "living decay." The male doctors in Fairfield (there was one female surgeon) accepted the conventional wisdom about menopause as the end of a woman's usefulness, the shutting down of her essential nature, a final empty stage before the end. The clock took away freshness, the ability to be swept up in sudden emotion, an eagerness for the next pleasure.

122

Busy with an active life, Mid had not focused on how middle age would affect her sense of self and her relationship with Oscar after the last of the children left home. It would be just the two of them, and she was not really a complete person. While Oscar, inspired by renewed interest in the arts (and artists!), seemed ready to explode with renewed energy, Mid felt she was imploding under the weight of time.

# Chapter Seventeen: Chores

Mid enjoyed visiting Charlotte Miller, though conversation with her always had to be carried on around farm chores--churning butter, straining milk, canning vegetables. Her husband, Harold, had grown up on a farm in Indiana; and, though he was now chair of a university physics department, he couldn't leave behind the rhythms of his childhood.

"I wanted to ask you about your clock," Mid said when she called earlier. "I'd like to know its history before I see what I can do."

"Come by on your way to the grocery store." Charlotte knew Mid reserved Thursday afternoons for that task. While it was no longer necessary to keep to a rigid schedule of household chores, Mid continued the habit established when the children were little (there had been so much to do then, and Oscar was so little help): laundry (by hand) on Monday, dusting and sweeping on Tuesday, sewing on Wednesday, bookkeeping on Friday.

And, of course, every day involved making beds, putting away toys, and cooking, though Mid's work in the kitchen was made easier because Oscar's tastes were simple. Watching Charlotte do the same chores--plus get eggs from the chickens, milk the cow, work the vegetable garden--did make Mid admit that she was not suffering unduly.

Today she found her friend canning green beans. With only a floor fan to cool her, she was working at a table cluttered with jars, lids, and discarded bits of plant as steam rose around her from pots bubbling on the stove.

"So, you want to know about Mid Ben. It's one of three that came down in the family."

"'Mid Ben'? That's what you call the clock?"

"Yes. Harold's uncle inherited Big Ben, the grandfather clock in the hall of the old house, and his aunt got the small tambour one in her bedroom, Little Benny. So the cuckoo clock Harold has was called Mid Ben. All three were in one house long ago."

"If I take on fixing Mid Ben, then, I guess I'll working on myself--Mid." (Why did she have to think of the phrase "Has Been"?)

Charlotte laughed. "Women are always working on themselves, since we're never up to our husband's standards."

"Especially when we don't know what those standards are, or that they've suddenly been changed. How do we know how we should be?"

Charlotte wiped her brow with a cloth and reached for the oven mitts. "I'm pretty aware of myself as a hot person today! Would you be a dear and put a lid on each jar after I fill it?" She had cooked the cut beans for eight minutes and was pouring the mixture into pint jars.

"Sure." Mid took an apron off a peg by the door, and they worked together quietly, moving beans into jars and jars into the canning pot. With two large pots boiling--Charlotte wanted to do over twenty pints--the full process would take several hours.

"As for pleasing our husbands," Charlotte continued, "I've been thinking about something Richard was telling me the last time he was home." Ricky was the youngest of her three sons. His two brothers, older by ten and twelve years, had become physics professors like their father. Rick, a good friend of Curtis, had a tendency to rebel against his father.

Recalling that Curtis had assumed she would need looking after when he went back to school and Carol had gone into the Army, Mid said, "He and Curtis can offer interesting advice."

"Rick believes you heal the fractures in yourself when you fix a mechanical thing. If you forget about your own worries or your troubles, and focus on something outside the self--a clock, for instance--your mind comes to terms--unconsciously, I guess--with whatever has been troubling you. That's his justification for his model train obsession, I guess."

"So, if I concentrate on the making the clock run, I'll run better myself. Well, I admit that I've always turned to my knitting when I'm upset, but I thought it was to escape my problems. Now you're saying it may be the best way to deal with them."

"I try to do that even when the work is hard--and hot!" Again, she wiped her brow.

Charlotte often talked about the relentless pressure of sustaining their twenty-acre farm, with its small herd of sheep, one milk cow, a dozen chickens, and various dogs who, in theory, worked the sheep. (She was not counting as her responsibility cats dumped by the side of the road, mice eating the animal's feed, rabbits, and groundhogs making off with however much of Charlotte's garden they could.)

When the processing reached a stable boiling, Charlotte suggested they sit in the shade by the garden and enjoy the breeze. "I have a feeling you want to talk about more than clocks. Is it Carol and her joining up?"

"No, oddly. I have a lot of confidence in her. And I know when she's made up her mind, it's useless to try to change it. I was going to ask you about Ellie Newton. Is she okay?"

"I think she's relieved. It had taken her years to come to the realization that she couldn't be happy with Jack." Charlotte wiped the perspiration from her forearms with the dishcloth she'd taken from the kitchen. "And then more years to work up the courage to tell him. Well, you and I know what it's like to be married to scientists. They live in their own worlds."

Mid gazed across the garden and down to the pond. Curtis and Rick had spent many happy hours catching small perch from the shore. "They certainly do. But then, my father, a marine insurance adjuster, also kept his work mostly to himself."

"But I assume he stepped on boats, inspected cargo in person, had his hands on the business. Our men live in their heads, fantasy worlds of numbers and diagrams."

"So Eleanor wanted—what? a little more attention?"

"The attention all wives want--appreciation, praise. That other attention—she didn't want that anymore." Charlotte clucked her tongue. "And some say he started directing it elsewhere anyway."

Mid recalled Arthur James commenting on--what did he call it?--her "bottomness" and "topness." Some men reaching middle age were consumed with a desire to act like boys.

She stood up. "I'd better be going, still have the groceries to pick up and want to be home in time to cook. Is this all the canning you have to do today?"

"Yes, but, before I put Harold's dinner together, I have to feed the chickens and skim the cream off the milk." She laughed and rose as well. "Oh, well a farm woman's work is never done!"

"Don't you get so tired with—," Mid waved a hand at the barn, the sheep milling around it, the garden, "with all this that you just want to give it all up and come live in town?"

"I did when we first moved here. I didn't grow up on a farm, but I did spend several weeks each summer at my grandparents' in the country. They just let me and my cousins treat it like a vacation--swim in the creek, play in the loft, sleep on the screen porch. So I had a romantic view of rural life. The first few years after buying this land I went to bed every night bone tired."

"And now?"

"Now I've adjusted. There's something salutary about the routine, the changing of seasons, paying attention to rainfall, corn prices, temperature affecting crops. It's an ancient way of life, of course, and I feel connected to the past--even when I'm exhausted."

"Oscar only has bad memories of his grandparents' farm and his Swedish aunts and uncles'. He's glad his parents wanted him to rise, not to have work with his hands."

"I certainly take advantage of modern conveniences--the chest freezer; the tractor, of course; the medicines that cure an ailing lamb. After all, that's what our university is contributing to by producing engineers and scientists. But I'm still grateful to be grounded in this old way of life--even if, right now, I have to shoo you along so I can finish the day's chores."

That evening Mid imagined asking Oscar if he'd want to buy twenty acres in the country and raise goats. He could already hear his laughter. But she wanted to propose something the two of them could take on together, a project to occupy them and heal their inner fractures. Maybe he'd consider buying land at The Lake of the Ozarks and taking up sailing. She knew others who were thinking of this developing area as the place for their retirement home.

Oscar did like to claim his Scandinavian roots, boasting that his forbearers, the Vikings, were fearsome warriors and intrepid explorers. "We were here before your ancestors came along in the Mayflower," he'd told her when they were first dating.

Didn't she have a mailing about waterfront property in her stack of mail somewhere? The cover photo had caught her eyes, reminding her of Greenwood Lake, site of fond childhood memories. She would find it and surprise him with a proposal, a proposal so tantalizing he'd forget all about *Little Sheba* and Professor Baudin.

# Chapter Eighteen: Recreations

"Next summer," Mid suggested after dinner, "I'd like to spend some time with my mother, more than four or five days like we've done in the past because of all our obligations here. Carol will be in the Army, then, and the boys at school, so you wouldn't have to teach to earn extra money. What do you say to a decent vacation?"

Oscar, sitting in his customary recliner, fingered the keys on his saxophone. "I think I'm going to have get the pads on my horn replaced." He'd begun to test it out a few days earlier, saying he was too good a talent to hide from the rest of the world.

"I don't know anything about fixing up an old horn."

Mid had never played an instrument. She did take piano lessons briefly before she moved to Missouri, back when she was living with her mother and working. But she quickly recognized she was a better listener than musician. While Oscar had told her about his experience, she'd never heard him perform.

"The good thing is, this is a quality saxophone. I bet the newer ones are made with inferior material and craftsmanship, all to save money. My dad was always telling me about the shortcuts builders took, using more mass-produced parts rather than crafting them by hand. Probably the same with musical instruments."

Oscar's father had died several years earlier, Carl's wife six months before that. With Sadie gone, Carl didn't look after himself; and Mid often had to drive up to see about him or to take him to doctors. Despite knowing her for more than twenty years, he never confided in her. Even during these times his Scandinavian reserve was impenetrable.

"We could go the Finger Lakes, too, spend some time with my sister, Thel. You always like it by the water."

"You need to play an instrument regularly, just like driving your car. If it sits, parts dry out and stiffen up."

"*Stiffen up*," thought Mid. There were ways that applied to each of them as this stage in their lives. And one important way it didn't in his case—as least, she concluded unhappily, it hadn't happened in her recent experience.

"Remember when you took the boys canoeing out that one time in the wind? It was the wrong time to try to make it all the way across." Lake Canandaigua was over a mile wide at her sister's cottage, several times larger than New Jersey's Greenwood Lake where the Lacy sisters had spent summers growing up.

"Undertones, my cousins' band, used to play at a joint down by the river in Jeff City. I'm sure it's long gone by now. But, when it was really hot, with all the windows and the doors open, you could smell all sorts of foul things coming off the water. Well, when the cigar smoke and spilled beer were at moderate levels."

"It was a honky-tonk establishment?"

"'Establishment' is too fine a term. It was a dive where businessmen and politicians got drunk and met women of the night." He removed the mouthpiece and blew through it. "I was just an observer, of course — an observer and musician."

Oscar's half-smile made Mid wonder if he wasn't editing this account for her. Again, because they had the agreement not to talk about their respective romantic pasts, there were moments when she sensed gaps in her understanding of his past.

Of course, there were gaps in his knowledge of her life also. One involved the boy next door in Rutherford, who had waited so long and worked so hard to gain her appreciation. His Italian immigrant parents made him aware of the nature of fascism in their home country. He was among the first to volunteer, even before the United States went to war, and among the first to die when it did. By that time Mid had come to admire his commitment; and his memory led her to England and the driver's seat of a Clubmobile.

"Say, will they have music for some of the university plays next year? Maybe you could be in a small orchestra or a jazz combo."

"I don't know about that, but they will need to recruit actors for some of the roles. Not many engineering students have an interest in the theater."

"You did the voices for many of your radio dramas, didn't you? Maybe you could take a small role, just to help."

He pulled the saxophone apart, testing the cork padding at the joints with his finger. "That's the thing--we will probably have enough men, even with so many focusing on their studies. Where we anticipate problems is finding the women. We may have to see if there are faculty wives who are interested. Or female faculty."

Watching him put his instrument carefully back in the felt-lined case, she realized at that moment that Marsha Baudin would play Lola Delaney in *Come Back, Little Sheba*. And that the young blonde would be mesmerizing.

"My brother-in-law's moving his sailboat down to the Maryland Eastern shore, where they're building a retirement home. You've read all those books about the sea--*Moby Dick, Two Years Before the Mast, South Sea Tales*--you would enjoy going out on the Chesapeake Bay, I'm sure."

"Um-hm. Well, I'm going to call the chair of the music department, see if someone locally can restore this beauty for me." He closed the case, reclined his chair halfway, and pushed the remote button to cut on the television. Mid weighed working on her clock against knitting.

She knew that burying herself in projects kept her anxieties under control--or at least pushed to the back of her mind. Oscar's distraction, Curtis' infatuation, Suzanne's exceptional (Catholic) competence. The worst fears, though she wouldn't admit it, involved Carol.

She remembered with pride how her own father had put her on a train in Newark for the ride to Archer College in Baltimore. She travelled alone with a steamer trunk full of clothes (That same trunk now held old linen and served as another work surface in her utility room.)

The year before Mid left for Baltimore, her older sister had gone to Ithaca College, not nearly so far away. And her older brother had attended university in Boston, but dropped out to marry and begin what would prove a very successful banking career. Mid was the only child in the family to head off to a distant destination on her own.

Mid had seen both her sons go off to college, but somehow that was not as hard as she had imagined. Men were supposed to strike out on their own. She sometimes worried that, because Oscar had lived with his parents while going to school, he might have been less prepared to adapt to change later in life. And perhaps he'd failed to prepare his children adequately.

As a college student in Baltimore, she had never thought about how her mother might feel back at the Ridge Road house in Rutherford--at least until Mid's father passed away at a relatively young age. History, this time with Mid as the mother left at home, was repeating itself.

Years later, after her father was gone, she had abandoned her mother a second time to come to Missouri. Of course, the families of one sister and brother had moved close, and Ethel was happy in a new home next door to the small church she'd help found in upstate New Jersey. Who shared Mid's home with her now? An abstracted and distracted husband, irregular letters from her two sons, a clock she still couldn't get to chime.

She wondered if she should make a special effort to contact Ellie Newton, just separated from her husband. Both might need friends, or even confidantes. They were, after all, neighbors in Middlecourt, Ellie living around the turn and up the hill. Their backyards were separated by only one other house and a vacant lot.

On her worktable she found the brochure for "Avalon Lake Homes," a development for "retirees and successful families that can afford a vacation getaway." She couldn't tell if Oscar would laugh at the Camelot imagery against an Ozark background or be drawn to the romance of Arthurian legend. Still, she decided to plot an excursion and test his reaction.

On an inside page she studied a knight of the Round Table on his valiant steed, lance upright and sword hanging down from the saddle. To one side a fair maiden in flowing robes offered her handkerchief to the man who would fight for her. Mid could not imagine what dragon or hireling of Mordred would emerge from the Missouri woods. She did, however, fear Morgan le Fay tempting an unsuspecting hero to her bed.

Looking again, Mid thought the knight a bit slight in build and his posture on the horse less aggressive than appropriate either for jousting or battle. If she lifted the visor and saw the warrior's face, whose countenance would she find? Her heart skipped a beat when her mind's eye saw Carol's face framed in cold metal.

# Chapter Nineteen: Spaces

Carol's orders seemed to be written in code. Of course, the time (such and such an hour on the certain day of this month in the year of) and the place to report (Selective Service Office, this number on that street in St. Louis) were straightforward; but notes like "5-HQ FILE, 5-MR CLK 1-AFEES TRANS CLK" made no sense to Mid.

When she had joined the Red Cross thirty years before, paperwork was kept to a minimum. She believed that had been because of the cost of paper, preparation, and duplication, as well as the primitive state of an evolving bureaucracy. Perhaps also in a time of national crisis people concentrated more on getting the job done.

At any rate, the multiple pages of mimeographed material bound to a piece of boxboard with a metal clasp took the place of Carol's remarkable academic transcripts over twelve years of schooling. And the young woman who boarded the bus in Fairfield with a single duffle bag of belongings left behind her parents' memories of a girl who had brought joy and pride to them at every stage of her young life.

She insisted she take this journey alone and that there be no tears from father, mother, or brother

(Louis would say goodbye in St. Louis); and there were none--until that night.

"Why am I taking this so hard?" Mid asked Oscar one evening. He had wandered out to the utility room in between television shows. Curtis was again out with Sarah, though his departure from home was only days away as well. "And, she added, "why are you so calm?"

Mid also wished Carol's brothers had tried harder to dissuade her from the decision to enlist; but they seemed to be caught up in their own lives and willing to grant their sister the right to make her own decisions.

"Has the television screen looked blurry to you lately?" Oscar asked. She remembered that he had been squinting at it during the evening news, turning his head to view it from different angles. But his eyesight had always been weak, so she hadn't worried.

"No more than usual. I mean, there's snow, static, I guess."

"Maybe my eyes are just tired," Oscar admitted, taking off his glasses and using his handkerchief to clean them.

Mid had not worn glasses until she was over forty. Now, a bit farsighted, she just needed them for reading, knitting, and clock repair (her present occupation). "I remember going away from Mother's little house in the country, that time I went overseas. It didn't occur to me that anyone would worry, with the men being the ones who had to do the fighting."

"I guess it depended on where you were going. There was a girl I knew back in Salinas who volunteered to go to China when they were at war with Japan. She was lucky to get away alive. Nice girl, Betty Devine. I wonder what happened to her."

"Don't you wonder what will happen to your own daughter? Walter Cronkite reported the other night that thousands of American advisers are being committed to the fighting in South Vietnam."

"Oh, that will be over by the time Carol finishes her training. And she'll be in some headquarters building decoding enemy messages--or the bad writing of her superiors."

Mid studied the wheels and gears of her family clock's chiming mechanism. When the central arbor turned the minute hand up to twelve, a cam lifted the warning lever and the gears made a half turn. They were held in place there until, a few minutes later, the counting lever was supposed to rise and chiming began. Mid's problem was that the counting lever went up but the wheels stayed still. The system was stuck somewhere.

"Remember how, when we met, you were so sure America would stay out of the war? We were just going to live our life together--work until we had some savings, you would go on to graduate school, I would start to have babies."

Mid studied the clock mechanism, suspended on the frame she had constructed in order to make adjustments.

"That's what we did," he said, "though it's true we had to delay a few years while I worked for the Navy. Still, we did what we wanted."

Mid knew he felt as if he were treading water during the war. "We were fortunate. You had the chance to use your gifts helping the nation as a researcher, then return to teaching. It's going to be a few years at least before we find out if Carol returns to—to what she's best at."

Mid realized she meant what she, Carol's mother, thought her daughter was "best at." Mid had constructed a future for her daughter drawn in part from her own frustrations as a young woman. In college, working with a gifted female researcher, she had anticipated advancing in the medical field. Her father's early death, the nation's gearing up for war, and the limited opportunities for professional women diverted her into a different path.

"She's like me--good at too many things. Here I've been slaving away at theoretical physics for twenty years when I could have been playing Charlie Parker tunes!"

Mid understood now that, before and during the war years, a structure had been in place within which her talents could find only limited opportunities. Given all the talk about women's liberation today, though, and the Cold War in a seemingly permanent stalemate, all her children ought to be able to pursue their dreams. Like Okies in the Depression, they could pack up and move down Route 66 to new opportunities; but unlike Steinbeck's unlucky travelers, they would achieve a new prosperity and a deeper happiness. This summer Mid felt they were all being deflected onto less fulfilling paths.

Tentatively, she pushed the top gear wheel with her forefinger. The gears spun, the hammer lifted and fell on the chime. *Ah-ha*, she thought. *The lift lever is freeing the gear, but something else is stopping it.*

She heard Oscar playing his saxophone; scales and arpeggios were skillfully sent floating from the den. He must have wandered off as she reminisced. It was a pattern for their evenings these days; he back there with his music and reading, she out here with her hobbies. When they had first been married, they did everything together--played cards, went for walks, saw movies.

Even when the kids came along, except for his work, they were always together. For years they listened to the radio in the evenings, then watched television as a couple. Where their tastes differed, she pulled out her yarns and needles, turning out baby sweaters, mittens, scarfs while he was engaged in westerns, spy shows, who-done-its. But they were in the same room.

Usually Oscar played sheet music he'd saved from his college years. At times he would improvise, recalling show tunes and jazz favorites from the 1930s. Mid assumed he was recalling performances at college and with his cousins. He was, she had to admit, quite good. Maybe he should have pursued another career!

Tonight he moved into a mournful, slow tune she didn't recognize. It reminded her, though, of the dream scene in *Come Back, Little Sheba*. Lola tells Doc how she dreamed of going to the Olympics. Her father was in charge, and, after one competitor was disqualified, the young Doc came out to throw the javelin. He threw it so far into the sky it didn't come down.

From her ladies bridge group Mid knew other couples their age spent less and less time together at home. And it often got worse rather than better after the children went away. The once noisy house became more still, and the inhabitants more sedentary. No one needed help with school projects, the doors didn't slam shut as teenagers raced in or out, there was no argument about who was next in the bathroom.

Maybe it had been made worse for the Lindblooms by their moving from a small house with small rooms to a large ranch house spread across half an acre. Right now they were at opposite ends of their home.

Each house on this street was also at least twice as far from the next as houses were in The Circle. While they used to chat with neighbors from their front stoop or across the fence, now the backyard patio where they sat with coffee was shielded from passersby by lattices.

Oscar's sad song continued, wandering down the hall and through the den and kitchen like smoke from a swamp fire with no visible flame at the source. Mid recalled how Lola in her dream found her lost dog Sheba in the middle of the Olympic stadium, dead and covered in dirt. Doc, listening to Lola's account, concluded only that dreams are strange.

In the movie version, Burt Lancaster is handsome, even though he's lost confidence and purpose. Shirley Booth is middle-aged, a little plump, wearing plain dresses. As she tells her dream, Lola and Doc are in a tiny kitchen, she working at the stove and he sitting at a small table. At least they are together.

Mid decided to walk up to Ellie Newton's house. She could go out the door onto the patio, cross two back yards, and be at her friend's screened porch in five minutes. Should she tell Oscar, leave him a note, or just go? It was probable he would never know she had been gone.

# Chapter Twenty: Directions

An hour and a half later, Mid returned to find the phone ringing in the kitchen. It was Louis calling from St. Louis to say he was thinking of dropping out of law school. After the initial shock, Mid managed to ask, "There's a reason?"

"Yes. What I've been doing this summer with the firm has confirmed it."

"It's not interesting enough? You know that's always the way it is when you're getting started in a profession. You're at the bottom and have to take on the boring, mundane tasks." Mid wished Oscar would pick up in the den. His recliner in the family room was empty.

"It's not that. It's what the work involves. And how the firm earns its money. Everything is geared to turning a profit--what clients we seek out, what cases we take on. There don't seem to be any—um—or enough good principles that guide us."

Mid took a Kleenex from the kitchen counter and wiped the sweat from her forehead. "You're not used to the business model, that's true. My father was in marine insurance, but he died so young you never had a chance to know him. And academics like your dad don't think of how the institution's bills get paid. Give it time."

"I think a year's a pretty good length of time. When I ask where I've come in twelve months, I can't see it as progress. I've studied a framework of rules meant to keep order; but what future good can get done within that order is never considered."

Mid walked across the kitchen holding the phone. It's long line allowed her to step through the open doorway into the family room. She hoped that raising her voice would rouse Oscar. "Well, what would you do if you weren't in law school? You might be postponing the problem of finding your place while losing the advantages of training in a profession."

There was a pause, and Mid felt he might be covering the receiver with his hand and talking to someone else. "Actually, I've been looking into a different program, one that involves values beyond simply making a living. There's a good theology program at Concordia."

"Theology? Ah. Well, you know your father isn't going to be enthusiastic about that. And how would you pay for it?"

Another pause, this one longer. "I've put away some money this summer—and there are ways to live more cheaply--you know, share expenses. Anyway, I don't have to make a decision for another month. I just wanted you to know I was thinking about it. Nothing's definite."

146

Mid looked across the family room to the double glass patio doors. Oscar usually closed the curtains after supper, though shrubbery blocked anyone from seeing in. Tonight the curtains were still pulled back and Mid could see herself reflected in the glass.

Looking at the slumped figure in a worn dress, she thought, "That woman is old!" She could see several pieces of hair hanging loose, one plastered to her forehead with the heat. A hand was holding on to the doorjamb, almost as if its owner needed support to stand up. The other hand looked as if it might be dragged down by the weight of the phone.

She heard the front door open; Curtis came in. She decided to leave things with Louis where they were. "I'll talk with your father."

To her younger son, the jokester who would cheer her up, she said, "Have a nice night?"

"We did. We got together with Rick and his girlfriend--did you know he was in town?--and had good talks about—about everything, I guess."

"Baseball? I know he loves the Cards."

"Well, some, but they seem to be in a slump, barely at .500 and not gaining on the division leaders. No, we got to talking about the news, what's happening in some cities."

"There are riots, aren't there?" She put the phone back on the hook and sat down at the small kitchen table while Curtis opened the refrigerator.

As hard as Mid tried this summer to have regular family meals, everyone worked on his or her own schedule. Carol had been getting up before dawn, Curtis slept till noon on weekends. Oscar woke up during the night restless and ate snacks. Everything was out of sync.

"Right. People are getting killed, and they may send soldiers in some places."

"There's fried chicken in a bowl. And a bit of fruit. Did you have a decent supper?"

"Oh, you know. We get things at the Maid Rite, shakes, fries. Sometimes we're caught up in other things. Say, what would you say to my transferring schools after this year? You know, to get in a program Westminster doesn't have."

"Let me get your father out here." She almost bolted down the hall. "He'll want to hear." In a moment she came back. "Uh, he's not here. Must have gone out to — get something."

This never happened. When Oscar arrived home at the end of the day, he ate, napped, watched television, worked, or read in the den. Mid spoke to Curtis in a dazed state. "What program would you be looking for?"

"Um, it's called different things at different schools."

"Okay. Tell me some of the names."

"Well, you can have 'black studies' or 'ethnic culture studies' or 'women studies.' It's really an effort to expand the range of traditional disciplines."

"I don't understand."

"Instead of studying the history written by white men about white men, for instance, you consider the contributions of women--Carrie Nation, Sojourner Truth, Madame Curie. There's Frederick Douglass, of course, and George Washington Carver, so men are important, too."

"Aren't they already studied? I seem to remember—" She trailed off.

"They're mentioned, but mostly in passing. A lot of history is defined by monarchs and wars, not by what ordinary people have done. Plus, there's much too much emphasis on British and American culture. We should be studying Russian authors and Chinese writers. The current college curriculum is so narrow. And it hasn't changed in decades."

Mid wanted to say there were probably good reasons it hadn't changed: history was history. But the evening's events had made her dizzy. "You talk this over with your father. It's time for me to go to bed." She left him pulling a handful of fig newtons from the cookie jar.

In the quiet of her room she sat in front of her dresser and studied herself in the mirror. Their bedroom furniture of dressers and bed had belonged to her parents, shipped out by Mid's older brother, who was aware how difficult life was on a beginning professor's salary. By her hands lay the ivory hand mirror, hairbrushes, and combs her mother had used.

She picked up a comb to lift her hair and let air to her scalp. While Oscar had agreed to buy this house, he insisted they could not afford air conditioning. Mid had put their old exhaust fan on a stand in the utility room, and it drew air through the length of the house. But tonight she felt she would never cool off.

"Am I in the same situation as Ellie Newton?" she asked herself. Her friend had told her she still loved her husband but felt he had become indifferent to her, especially after the children were gone. He didn't dislike her or like her; he tolerated her but did nothing with her. She felt she was neither divorced nor married, dangling in some suspended state, weightless as a person would be in space, unable to move forward, back, or to the side.

"So, I've asked him to leave, Mid," she explained. I'm not sure what I'll do, whether I'll stay here, move closer to one of the kids, or go off on my own somewhere."

"What does he say?"

She folded the napkin she'd gotten out when she offered Mid cookies. "He says it doesn't matter to him. He'll move out, get an apartment; I can have the house."

Mid set the glass of iced tea on the table. "He's not—there's no one else, is there?"

"He says no. And, in this town, generally people find out. At least no one has spoken to me. Anyway,

150

he goes in to teach; he works in the lab; he watches television. It's—it's an empty life for me. There's nothing to look forward to. When I think back, the path we traveled doesn't seem to have led anywhere."

Mid promised to be a better friend and said she hoped Ellie would stay in the house so they could get together often. And she meant it. At home in her room, she wondered if she would end up needing Ellie more than Ellie would need her.

She heard the television, but knew Curtis was probably the one who had turned it on. Oscar had tired of the *Tonight Show* and most nights retired to his study or to bed. She decided to tiptoe down the hall, though, just in case and see.

Since the door to Oscar's den was open, she looked in. The lamp by his desk was on and she could see a letter on top of a paperback, folded open and lying on its back. Seeing the letterhead of Enchantment College, she leaned down to read it. The letter "strongly urged" Oscar to apply for the position of Chairman, Department of Science.

# Interlude: Ups and Downs

Somewhere in the mid-1950s, a decade before the crisis in the Lindbloom marriage, the family took the 1955 Ambassador to Salinas, Kansas, to visit the haunts of Oscar's youth. He made no contact with his Swedish relatives living in nearby Assyria but did seek out his best friend growing up, Bob Peterson. The high point of the visit--literally and figuratively--was the B-47s taking off and landing at Smokey Hill Air Force Base just outside of town.

"Watching those Stratojets come and go is worth the price of admission," boasted Bob. He had met them at their motel and was going to lead them to the Middle of America restaurant, known for its ribs and corn on the cob.

"It costs?" asked Louis, at that time interested in the politics of the Cold War and the intricacies of air defense systems.

"Not a penny," laughed Bob. "We drive your dad's luxury sedan out on the dusty prairie, park off a country lane outside the fence, and watch from our luxury seats."

This was the first of many jokes he would make about the new Nash. It had replaced the one lost in an accident, and Oscar was extra cautious about where he took it.

Bob went on. "The best time is dusk, with planes silhouetted against the spreading sunset. Sometimes late at night their sonic booms wake us up, and we feel we're under assault."

"Sonic booms?" asked Carol.

Bob explained, "When a plane travels faster than the speed of sound. shock waves are created. The plane breaking through that barrier creates a sound like an explosion."

"I want to see where Dad learned to swim," said Curtis, intrigued by the idea that his father was once a boy.

Bob turned to Oscar. "Have you been telling them about how your father pitched you into the Salinas River and said, 'There you go now, boy.'"

"Of course. The same way you're going to tell them we walked to school barefoot in the snow, uphill both ways in a flat prairie town."

Bob, who had never married, had no children on which to inflict such stories. However, he had a longtime girlfriend, Alice, with whom he had breakfast every morning at the Crossroads Diner and with whom he went to concerts, plays, lectures. However, they kept separate homes in what Oscar believed was a chaste relationship.

Mid felt there had to be some long ago moment in their romance when Bob was ready to pop the question, but didn't. Now, she believed, he looked back sadly at that lost chance.

"Let's get something to eat right now," she advised, recognizing that she would have to keep this group moving. "We can watch the show tomorrow night." This whole venture was not her idea of a family vacation; but it had seemed important to her husband.

Oscar had received an early promotion that spring, based on good teaching and outstanding research. None of his colleagues understood his work in theoretical physics, but his papers were beginning to be accepted in the top tier of scholarly journals. For Harold Miller, the chair, young Dr. Lindbloom represented the institution's future as the college evolved into a university. The trip to Kansas was Mid's concession to Oscar's success. She didn't see it at the time as a first backward glance at his rise to the present.

Busy with housework and raising children, Mid had little leisure to think of vacations or travel that year. Two recent summers had been spent at the national laboratory in Oak Ridge, Tennessee; and she had been in charge of closing up the house on Limestone, packing enough to last them for ten weeks in a rented apartment, and entertaining little children while their father was outsmarting the Russians in weapons development.

She'd hoped they might go back east for a visit with her family. But Oscar pointed out her mother had spent two weeks with them the summer before. And the expense of such a trip would be a strain, even with the raise in pay he was to receive in the next year.

If the family were going west, Mid would have preferred traveling down Route 66, especially as it was sure to be replaced by this Eisenhower's national highway system. But they went west and north through Kansas City and on to countryside that held little interest for her and friends she had only heard about.

While Oscar was working during the war, undertaking graduate study, and then starting out as a young faculty member, Mid had had three children in rapid succession. In that busy time there had been few opportunities to reconnect with their respective pasts. And she recognized quickly that Oscar, always competitive, was measuring his current status with that of his contemporaries growing up.

His two closest friends had never left Kansas and pursued conventional roles. She liked Bob, but another friend, whom Oscar had never mentioned, troubled her. Bob said they would enjoy seeing his farm outside of town.

After they'd arrived and gone through the introductions, Marvin Battle offered genially, "Come see the game room." The men all trooped downstairs, while Mrs. Battle prepared drinks. She told Mid to go ahead, too; she didn't need help.

In the basement, Curtis exclaimed, "A table tennis table!" He was always ready for play.

Louis looked at the small room in one corner enclosed by cinder blocks and featuring an especially solid-looking door. "Is that a — um — bomb shelter?"

"It is," Marvin admitted.

Carol and Curtis had picked up ping-pong paddles at opposite ends of the table and were sending questioning looks toward their parents. Marvin smiled, "By all means. Just don't challenge your dad. He was pretty good in his day."

Mid was studying some fine wooden cases on a wall beside a heavy steel door. "What's stored here? Looks too elegant for canning."

"Most of our food supplies are inside the shelter. What we've got here," he gestured toward the padlocked cases, "are what will keep others out."

"Guns?" asked Louis.

"Well, whatever might be necessary."

Marvin pulled her and Oscar aside. "We worry about the Reds overseas, of course. But what concerns me just as much is the government. They've been — infiltrated."

"*Our* government?"

Oscar stepped in. "That's a matter for discussion another day, right? I'm on vacation right now. Tell me about the business, Marvin. I understand it's still booming."

Marvin ran a cement factory. His wife complained for years that he spent all his time at work, so three years ago he bought twenty acres in the

156

country, built this house, and started farming on a modest scale. Now she said he worked all day and night. They had no children.

The rest of the visit with Marvin and Faye was pleasant, but Mid couldn't get the vision of his basement armory out of her mind. She'd followed the McCarthy hearings, but didn't believe her own government had been taken over from the inside. Nor that armed citizens would have to protect their homes against fellow countrymen.

Oscar later told her this was not the Marvin he'd grown up with. And they let Bob and Alice--always referred to as his "lady friend"--propose the remainder of their itinerary.

Parked at dusk on the prairie outside Smokey Hill Air Force Base, Mid experienced a sense of the land's greatness. A gentle wind made sweeping waves in the tender wheat. And the sky was limitless. Of course, the sounds belonged to humans.

"The planes will go as far as the other side of the world," Bob told them. They can refuel in air, reach a target, return without ever touching ground. No other country has this."

Louis said, "I guess that's why they take off at night, to circle the globe."

"Here it goes!" said Curtis. To their right, they saw the six bright red circles of jet engine burn even brighter, heard their roar increase from loud to deafening, watched the swept-wing grey bird lumber down the runway. Another moved into place behind it, a line of the fleet making their way from hangars. One could take off every fifteen seconds.

"What do they carry?" asked Carol.

"Atomic bombs," Oscar said softly. "Enough to destroy whole cities."

"The world as we know it," added Mid.

"They keep the world we know safe," argued Bob. "So long as we have these patrolling the skies, your children can grow up and prosper in a peaceful world."

In one sense he was right. But after Sputnik was put in orbit by Russia, they would all wonder when we'd lost the lead to a rival super power. Even worse was the haunting suspicion that, like all empires, America's could be beginning to crumble.

# Volume Three: Spring

# Chapter Twenty-one:
# Worlds

On the night Mid walked out of the house to visit Ellie Newton, the Lindblooms' phone rang. Oscar tried to ignore it. Aware of his tendency to shut himself off, Mid had insisted on putting an extension in his study. He usually muted the ringer, but she must have turned it up earlier in the day. When it wouldn't stop, he picked up the receiver.

"Lindbloom residence."

"It's Marsha—Professor Baudin." Her voice was low, and she seemed shaken.

"Oh, uh—hello."

"I need a favor."

Instinctively, Oscar wanted to call Mid. She was the one who did favors. And he was uneasy in his relationship with this young woman. "I see. Is there a problem at the university—?"

"No."

There was muffled conversation in the background, and he felt she was holding the phone close.

"Oscar, I need a ride from the train station, from someone who can keep this quiet."

Oscar's mind was racing. He put his hand over the receiver, opened the door into the hall, and listened to see if he could hear Mid anywhere close.

"Uh, well, I suppose I can. You're at the station now?"

"Yes. I'm so sorry about this. I thought I could walk back to my apartment, but—but I'm not feeling so well. If you could possibly do this for me, I will be so very grateful."

"Okay. I'll be there as quickly as I can."

Oscar's plan was to get Mid to go with him. He had no idea why he was the one Marsha was calling; and he couldn't imagine what had put her at the train station at night so weak she couldn't walk. And why not call a cab? He should have asked her more questions.

When she'd called, he'd been in the middle of Edgar Rice Burroughs' *A Princess of Mars*. In the last year he found himself reading some of his favorite books over and over. Rather than plunge into mathematical formulas involving the property of liquids, he would scan his bookshelves and pull down a familiar novel. Tonight he was reading for his own pleasure, but also with an idea of helping Roger Stone get past the current block in his dissertation.

Mid was not in the family room or the utility room. An episode of *I Dream of Jeannie* was playing to no one in the family room. He and Curtis were both intrigued by the amazingly tiny waist and the bare, bellybutton-less midriff of Barbara Eden. But he couldn't stop now to fantasize about the genie in the bottle.

Oscar retraced his steps to their bedroom. Not there or in their bathroom. She wouldn't be out on the patio, where mosquitoes were waiting. He went back through family room and utility room to the garage-- both cars there, the door down. While it seemed unlikely, she might have gone for a walk. Perhaps a neighbor had come to the door and asked for her?

Finally, Oscar decided he would have to go on his own. On his way to the front door he heard Jeannie telling "Master" if he wasn't nicer to her, she would use her magic to return them to a deserted island in the middle of the Pacific.

It took Oscar less than ten minutes to drive downtown. As he rode, his thoughts wandered back to John Carter of Mars. Burrough's fictional hero often had to rescue maidens in distress. An ex-Confederate soldier who went west to search for gold, Carter had died in an Arizona cave. Resurrected somehow, he was transported to the planet of war. The lesser gravity gave him amazing physical powers. He became a great warrior and won the heart of Dejah Thoris, Princess of Mars.

Oscar's star pupil, Roger Stone, was a similarly gifted athlete on earth. At six-foot-six, he played football, ran track, and, of course, excelled in basketball. He even made it to the state high school wrestling finals after taking up the sport in his senior year on a bet from the coach. But his greatest abilities were intellectual; and finishing his undergraduate degree in three years at UC Berkeley, he had accepted a fellowship at the South Central to be closer his family in West Plains, Missouri.

He was the most promising candidate in the physics Ph.D. program at a time when the university was striving to establish itself as a research institution. While the department had awarded a number of doctorates in recent years, most were in applied fields, where state and national funding was available and the job prospect promising. To reach a higher tier, they wanted to produce a few distinguished theorists. And Oscar was the professor who had the ability to direct such individuals. Roger, however, was at the moment stumped in his work.

Marsha Baudin sat on a bench against the outside wall of the train station, a small black bag beside her. Pulling into a parking place, Oscar could see from her slumped posture and the strain in her face that she was not well. Getting out of the car, he said, "Let me help you."

She stretched out a hand. Without his arm, she might not have been able to get up. "You are so kind."

"What happened? Were you hurt getting on the train?"

"No. I went to Chicago for—a surgical procedure. It was supposed to be simple--I was supposed to go in and come out."

"Chicago?"

He had gotten her to the passenger side of the car and was holding the door open. But she hesitated, as if

163

it was too painful to move. "Are your seats leather?" she asked.

"Ah, yes. It's standard. . on this car." While Oscar was proud to drive his Jaguar sedan, he didn't like to boast. There wasn't another one in Fairfield, and it still had that new car smell.

Marsha remained still. "Will you open my bag, please? There's a towel on top. Please spread it on the seat. I wouldn't want to have an accident on such nice upholstery."

"Are you sure you don't need to go to a friend's? Or even the hospital. You—you are awfully pale."

"I'll be fine once I'm home. My landlady's there. You've been so kind. Please, it's not far--1015 Fairfield Street. I have an apartment on the bottom floor." Oscar did what she asked, but in his mind recorded a dozen questions he would ask Mid when he got home.

After he had helped her out of the car, up the sidewalk, and through the front door, she asked. "Could you walk me to the bedroom? The bath's right next door; I'll be okay there."

Oscar helped her to sit on the edge of the bed, putting her bag beside her. He tried not to look at pictures on the dresser or books on the bedside table. "Should I call your landlady?"

"Mrs. LaRoche is just upstairs; she'll come help me if I need something. She's nearly 90, and I didn't want to ask her to drive at night. I also didn't want to explain—where I've been."

Oscar knew he shouldn't inquire why she'd gone to Chicago--if indeed Chicago had been her true destination. (He wasn't sure he would later want to explain to many people where *he'd* been this evening!) After asking again if there was anything else he could do, anyone he should call, he reminded her that she had his phone number and let himself out.

The unexpected events of the night did not present the kind of straightforward challenges John Carter faced on Mars: giant green men threatening to chop his head off, palace treachery by those who wanted to steal a kingdom, seductive women who planned to entrap him and destroy his relationship with Dejah Thoris. Well, maybe this last was similar to Oscar's plight.

He suspected Mid resented his involvement in the emerging university drama program. She wanted the two of them to take up new interests together. But picking up his old love for literature--as well as playing the saxophone again--made him feel young and excited about the future. It didn't seem that Mid shared these interests. Explaining to her why Marsha chose him to help her tonight was going to take some skill.

The situation was more unsettling than challenges in his own research or Roger's dissertation. Both involved complex mathematical calculations, theories of matter that shifted with each new experimental discovery, rival schools of thought gaining or losing credibility in the profession. But Oscar always felt safe with numbers, underlying rules of order, the rigid demands of argument and proof. Finding himself alone in an attractive woman's bedroom required a subtlety of thought he hadn't had to employ in many years.

He thought of John Carter at one point in Burroughs' saga being brought back to earth, millions of miles from the world and woman he loves. Trapped in an Arizona cave he cannot fathom the path forward across a "cacti-studded valley" and beneath a moon and sky that "were not of Mars."

Parked in the garage of his house on Middlecourt, Oscar felt as if, once a talented writer for his college radio station, he had been transported to a world that at times seemed dead to him, then full of unexpected dangers. And, every once in a while, it was thrilling.

# Chapter Twenty-two: Falls

The minute he did it, Oscar knew telling Mid he had gone out to jump-start Roger's car was a bad idea. Not only was it unlikely he'd ever hook up the Jag's sophisticated electrical system to a '53 Ford pickup, but he'd later have to ask his student to back up his alibi. That could be awkward. A lie like this also had a tendency to expand and deepen over time.

Leaving Mid at work in the utility room, he found Curtis slumped on the sofa watching television. Settling in his recliner in the family room, he picked up his pipe. At the next commercial break between shows, he said to Curtis, "Let me ask you this. Are there limits to Jeannie's powers in that show?"

"Well, if she's corked inside her bottle, I don't think she can work her magic." Oscar noted that Curtis was working magic on a sandwich: making it disappear.

"But once out, she can do anything?"

"I guess so."

"It's sort of like Superman, then." Oscar was scooping his pipe into his tobacco pouch, punching tobacco down into the bowl with one finger. "At times there's no limit to how fast he can run, how high he can jump, how much he can lift. You'd think, then, there would never be a problem in the world he couldn't fix instantly. But not so. It's the same with Jeannie. Every week Tony gets into a predicament, and it takes thirty minutes to rescue him. It ought to be over in the blink of an eye--or eyes."

"Dad, I think you're reading too much into this. It's fantasy. Besides, Jeannie's beautiful."

"She does have quite a figure. What would happen if at one point Barbara Eden became pregnant? They'd have to replace her with another actress or make special outfits for her. A double could fill in in some scenes, and they could do a lot showing her only from the waist up."

As he talked, he lit his pipe. Oscar always used book matches, never a lighter, vaguely believing the fluid's fumes were unhealthy. He would tamp the burning contents down with a corner of the matchbook cover. He'd done this so many years, it was an unconscious routine.

"It wouldn't be a good idea for Jeannie to be carrying a child, would it?" said Curtis. "Viewers all across America would be outraged that a mythical creature and an astronaut, not married, did what it takes to make a baby. She'd be a fallen woman."

Oscar chuckled. "Well, I'm glad you and I had that little talk!" Then, as *Get Smart* began, he pushed his recliner back halfway and pretended to watch. He saw Mid pass through from the utility room on her way to the bedroom, but Oscar was thinking about tiny waists, including those of Marsha Baudin and of Curtis' current flame, Sarah Bridges.

168

He had never worried about Louis getting a girl in trouble. His older son, a conscientious student, had few dates in high school or college. And he was not one to take risks. Suzanne was the sensible girl Oscar expected Louis to end up with. Curtis, on the other hand, though as smart as his brother, was sometimes impetuous. And he was obviously attracted to this talented California girl. What did such a couple do on dates in this era?

Oscar's generation believed that physical relations with a "proper" woman put you on a path from which there was no turning back: marriage might come before or after, but the course was fixed. He knew this code was not absolute with his children's peers.

Carol had a friend who became pregnant in the middle of her senior year but succeeded in keeping it hidden until graduation. Then she married quickly and moved to Jefferson City. If her condition had been known, she would not have been allowed to continue coming to school. Carol was furious about this social convention, which penalized the woman when the man was as near to being a father as she was a mother; but Oscar accepted it as the norm.

Curtis had come in early tonight for a change, he realized, but there were many times when Oscar had fallen asleep before he heard Mid's Rambler pulling into the garage. He wondered whether this summer romance was going to continue into the school year. Was Curtis going to start over after another year with Sarah having become mother-to-be of his child?

Oscar, inspecting Agent 99, heroine of *Get Smart*, saw Mid pass by again, this time on her way out to her utility room. 99, too, had a good figure, though not as visible as Jeannie's in her skimpy outfit. Special Agent Maxwell Smart, the central figure of the show, was a bungler who had to be rescued by his partner in every episode. He was also easily duped by female agents of KAOS, an international organization of bad guys. Was Curtis aware of the danger in his current romance?

After he finished his pipe, Oscar went to his den, where he saw the letter from Enchantment College. He hadn't told Mid about the invitation to become a candidate for chairman, so he went back to the utility room where she was studying the innards of a cuckoo clock.

"Ah, another project under way," he noted. "Looks like a lot of parts." The works were out of the case and hanging on the frame she'd build for inspection and repair of a mechanism.

"It does. But I'm hoping it will be easier to restore than the Lacy clock. Charlotte said the last time she remembers, it was working. She just got irritated with its cuckooing and took it out to the barn. Harold, typical physicist, never noticed it was missing. Right now I'm just cleaning the parts, but it may be that time will start again for this little bird soon."

Oscar fingered one of the two small bellows inside the wooden case that made the bird sound. "Say, I've been meaning to mention that there's a college in Santa Fe apparently eager for me to apply for a position there."

She turned to look at him. "Oscar, we've just bought a new house, two of our children are close; why would we want to move halfway across the continent?"

"Yes, but you've been saying this is a time when we could pursue new interests. You always wanted to travel more, see different parts of the country. Isn't that how you ended up in Missouri after living most of your life back east?"

"That was in another life. We've been in Missouri for over a quarter of a century. And we can make changes in what we do here. For instance, I want to go check out Avalon Homes up at the Lake of the Ozarks. You can buy the lot and build on it later. But it would still be a place to get away for weekends. That's what my parents did camping out on Greenwood Lake."

"It would be a lot of work to build something."

"Oscar, if you don't want to consider a vacation campsite, why would you want to start over completely out west? Besides, who do you think has done most of the work in our moving across town? I contracted the movers, I packed the boxes, I supervised the children, and I'm still arranging clothes, furniture, appliances. I'm not about to do it all again."

He folded the letter up again. "I see your point. Still—" He turned to go back to his den, but then

171

added, "The department picnic is next weekend. Did I tell you?"

"Charlotte did. And it's always about this time, the weekend before classes begin."

"There will be softball as usual, on the Miller's sheep pasture. Will you watch this year?"

Oscar was a good athlete and loved the chance to step up to the plate. He'd been mad last year that Mid didn't join the other women on the porch to watch the game.

"As long as I don't need to help with the food."

"I heard that Roger will pitch this year. Oh, by the way, his truck wouldn't start tonight. I had to run out and help him get it started."

"I bet he'd let you borrow it now to carry supplies up to our lakeside campsite."

Oscar grunted and turned to leave. "I'll keep that in mind."

He didn't like to admit that he could neither hit nor throw the fastball as well as he once did; but each year he was determined to show the younger faculty that he was not completely over the hill. Tonight, he winced as he remembered challenging Curtis to a 100-yard dash back in the fall. That he'd lost, though not by much, was acceptable. That he'd fallen down was not.

Fortunately, it happened one evening, and there were no witnesses. But from a leaning start position, the two had collided with their first step. And Oscar, lighter now than his younger son, lost his balance and tumbled to the grass. Curtis apologized over and over, saying it was his fault; he'd lost his balance. Oscar insisted on a second try and afterwards concluded he'd been slowed by the effects of the fall. But perhaps it did mark a turning point on the road of aging.

Back in his study, he picked up *The Gods of Mars*, which opens with John Carter trapped in the Valley of Dor. It would be many pages before the hero was reunited with Dejah Thoris, and Oscar didn't have the patience right now to read to that point. He began to concoct the alibi he would ask Roger to confirm. Then it occurred to him that Mid had never explained where she had been when he answered the call from Marsha.

# Chapter Twenty-three: Hoops

Oscar knew that Roger played in a pick-up basketball game every Sunday, even in the summer. So, he planned to tell Mid he needed to run over to the library; then he'd drop by the gym and explain the situation with Marsha Baudin to his student.

He would have done all this more calmly if he hadn't been the first to take the call from Carol that morning. "Everything okay?" he asked, almost assuming that her intense military training had already been more than she'd anticipated.

"Roger that! I'm near the top of my class."

"In academic tests, that wouldn't surprise me a bit."

"That *and* in physical training. All that work I did with Aaron has paid off. The drill sergeant was kidding me the other day about going airborne."

"Your mother will want to hear all this. Let me get her from the patio." When she came in, he stepped out to allow a mother-daughter confidential talk.

Oscar had been quietly hoping that Carol was already discouraged by basic training. She'd been so idealistic about the military, he was sure she'd resent having to jump through hoops that meant nothing. He'd also read that drill sergeants harassed female recruits as harshly as males, breaking the spirit of many. And lots of people had to drop out for "medical reasons."

There would be a brief time of embarrassment, of course; but Carol could then start over, probably in January, as a freshman at the University of Missouri. She would do so well in the spring semester that she'd get scholarship money for the following year. Rather than the four-year false start of her enlistment, then, her professional life would have a brief gap that became invisible in just a few years.

Oscar viewed Mid's brief Red Cross tour during the war in the same light--a meaningless interruption. It was, he felt, analogous to the time he worked as a research associate for Dr. Bohns, his instructor at Salinas Wesleyan. Oscar's father had been injured and unable to work, so the son had to become the breadwinner. But when Carl was well again--and business picked up across the country near the end of the Depression--Oscar's life resumed its destined course. Or at least, that was what Oscar came to believe at the time. Recently, though, he had started to wonder if that two-year gap in his study might have been an opportunity he had overlooked.

During that time he fantasized becoming a jazz musician, joining up with one the big bands, touring the country, and being heard on the radio. He wouldn't necessarily stay on the road forever, but eventually settle down in some big city, give private lessons, play regularly in a local lounge. He had the talent.

He had also thought about studying architecture. While going to college was one path into that profession, another was to become an apprentice to an established architect. If he'd taken that second route, he probably would have seen the world; designed museums, churches, monuments; met wealthy and powerful men — well, and women.

What he'd chosen, he now realized, was the life of the mind and the security of family. While he was recognized by others with similar intellect, he had not earned great wealth, widespread fame, or public stature. He had spent years building mathematical models of things people could not touch, hear, or feel.

He was not going so far as to conclude that he had made wrong choices when, encouraged by his former professors and his boss at the state health agency, he decided to go on to graduate school in the field that helped his country win World War II. Weapons research was a significant part of the worldwide effort of Allied scientists and engineers to stop Germany and Japan from world domination.

Then, in the Cold War, it was assumed we needed more brilliant young men to bolster deterrence, stalemating the Soviet Union and Red China. So, he continued his research and his teaching in part as a patriotic duty. After the stalemate of Korea and this new unsettling involvement in Southeast Asia, though, some were arguing America had failed to understand a changing world. We were in a new game but playing with old rules, outdated strategies, and weapons designed for earlier conflicts.

Well, he'd given two decades to this demanding work, and now he had a right to begin exploring additional ways to use his talents.

"Are you going out today?" Mid asked, one hand on the doorjamb of his study.

"I do have to drop by the library. Do you need me to pick up something?"

"If you want your favorite oatmeal cookies, yes." She paused a moment. "How did Carol sound to you?"

"Too good, I'd say. She seems more enthusiastic about all this than I'd predicted."

"Yes. Well, zeal is good, but I think there are more tests to come. They want her to take advanced training in espionage as well as intelligence."

"You think they're going to have her parachuting in behind enemy lines or sneaking through the Iron Curtain? I wouldn't worry about that. She's destined for a desk job."

"I hope you're right. Well, don't forget the cookies."

He was happy that this errand would give him cover for his other mission. Like a secret agent himself, he had to hide his tracks.

Roger Stone had played as a walk-on with the freshman basketball team at Berkeley, finishing the season as a starter and getting a scholarship offer for the next three years. But he turned it down. He told

Oscar he was bored with regimented play, the minute-by-minute coaching, a complete lack of joy in the whole enterprise. And he wanted to study physics.

Watching him on the court today, Oscar could tell he was the best athlete out there, even though he was playing at half speed and some of the other graduate students had been on varsity teams. When he came over to sit in the bleachers beside Oscar, he smiled, "Wanna' get the next game with me? Two on two."

"Ordinarily I would, but today I'm on my way to and from. Have you got a minute?"

"Sure, as long as you're not asking me how the dissertation is going."

"I won't do that, though I do happen to have some oddball advice for you."

"Oh?"

"Yes, I've been stuck on my own summer project for the last week or so. Or I was until this morning. Woke up and the answer was staring me in the face. How had I missed it before!"

"I'm ready for an epiphany. I wake each morning knowing only that I'm right where I was the night before — or perhaps back three steps."

"Here's my suggestion, then: put the whole thing aside for a few days. Don't think about it, don't worry about it, don't admit it exists. Escape to another world."

"Go overseas?"

"No, just to Mars. I'm loaning you the first book of Edgar Rice Burroughs' John Carter books, *The Princess of Mars*. Here. Ever read it?"

"Never heard of it. It solves math problems? Fantasy beats physics?"

"No, not that. But sometimes you get so buried in your problem that you lose sight of the obvious. When that happens, I've learned, you need to turn your conscious mind to almost anything else, something unrelated. And, if you're like me, which I suspect, your unconscious mind will find an answer on its own. It's a trick of misdirection."

"Hmm." He inspected the dust-jacket, sword-wielding John Carter protecting a woman who looked like an Indian goddess. "Is the book any good?"

"It will take you away--not from all this—" he waved at the gym. "But all this." He pointed to Roger's head.

"Sounds worth a try. Thanks."

"Now, to ease my worries, I need a favor. Last night, completely unexpected, I got a call from Professor Baudin in the theater department. She needed a ride from the train station. For some reason, she wanted it kept a secret, some personal matter involving—her health. She didn't know who else to call."

"I see."

"So, I took her home, but, to protect her privacy, like she asked, I didn't explain all this to Mrs.

Lindbloom. I said, um, that you needed me to jump start your truck."

"Ah, so I'm your alibi."

"That term might make me uncomfortable, as there was nothing illegal or—clandestine—going on. But, well, you know that women are unable to resist gossip; and the story would spread. What would be the point? Men can be trusted to keep a confidence."

When Roger said, "Sure, got it. Your secret's safe with me," Oscar was relieved. But back home on Middlecourt Drive, he replayed the look on his friend's face and groaned.

# Chapter Twenty-four: Sons

When Oscar first learned about the Enchantment College position, he reread Willa Cather's 1925 *The Professor's House*, part of which is set in and around Santa Fe. Cather tells the story of a middle-aged college teacher and his wife preparing to move into a new house. The husband starts to question his entire life. Perhaps Oscar was doing the same thing.

Godfrey St. Peter begins to suspect his study of early Spanish exploration has been trivial in the grand scheme of things. And the fate of one of his prize students haunts him. Tom Outland had traveled to the American Southwest and fallen in love with its stark natural beauty, but he returned to participate in "the war to end all wars," which ended him.

Cather's central character had daughters, no son; so in some ways, he had adopted Tom Outland. Reading his pupil's journal, St. Peter wonders if, in devoting his own life to books, he failed to understand his homeland and its true heroes. Had St. Peter spent his adulthood looking backward at European history rather than forward to possible liberation from dead and deadening customs?

Thinking about the fictional professor, whose student represented a path not taken by his teacher, Oscar reviewed his own choices in the context of history. Did America, by entering the Great War two generations ago, push itself forward into a new era represented by the prosperity of the 1920s, a decade in which Oscar's father made a lot of money in construction? In the wake of Europe's losses, it did seem that America advanced as an industrial country and became a greater world power.

But that same event, going to war, might be viewed as a step backward: the new Eden was corrupted by a colonial mentality, which overvalued wealth, power, and status. Certainly the worldwide Depression of the 1930s, which nearly ruined Oscar's father, meant that the systems of democracy and capitalism had not solved all social problems.

Oscar had taken for granted that his research and the applied skills of his students in the 1940s and '50s added to the strength of a benevolent superpower. But had his efforts aided the nation's original goals of freedom, peace, the rights of man? Or did they add another chapter to the history of empires that sought dominance for their own sake? Back in his study after his talk with Roger, Oscar picked up the letter from Enchantment. Was it a message to him: "Go west, young man, go west"? Also on his desk was a letter in which Louis expanded on his concerns about pursuing a career in law. Oscar folded both letters up and went to find Mid.

"What are we having for dinner?" he asked. "The usual Sunday pot roast?" She was in her workshop.

"Did you smell anything cooking on your way out here?"

"Well, no. I was just assuming. Of course, it's only you and me, isn't it? Curtis will be with Whatshername."

"Sarah, yes. She has him under her thumb. Anyway, I decided to give myself a day off from cooking. We have leftovers, that meatloaf from Friday. Charlotte brought by some fresh corn on the cob, though, and you should have your cookies."

Oscar winced. "You know, I got so caught up in this article at the library, I forgot it."

She looked up from her clock's wooden cuckoo bird, which she was repainting. "I see you looked at Louis' letter. What do you think?"

"I still think he'll stay on. Everyone says the second year of law school is more interesting."

"Did you read the paragraph about 'instruction'?"

"'Instruction'? Wasn't he just talking about classes?"

"He's talking about becoming a Catholic, taking formal 'instruction' in that faith."

"Ah! I guess I didn't pick up on that."

Mid turned back to her work. Oscar stood for a moment, rereading the letter. Then he wandered toward his study.

His son might be more serious about Suzanne than Oscar had suspected; perhaps he was even thinking of proposing marriage. Oscar assumed she would not accept a non-Catholic, though a lot of converts in such cases never become practicing churchgoers. Still, their children would be baptized in the church and probably go to Catholic schools. This move would shape the rest of Louis' life.

Even after he had fallen in love with Mid, he projected the future based on his professional career--work, graduate school, university position, research opportunities. Mid would simply accompany him down that road, not change the direction. But he remembered being shocked when she became pregnant so quickly. Suddenly, they had to prepare for a different future, make wise choices to ensure the family's wellbeing, think about how and where to raise children.

It had occurred to him much too late that the nine months of her pregnancy should have educated him--"instructed" him, he chuckled--about that reality. Changes in Mid's mood, morning sickness, binge eating, and tiredness were telling him that the future was not to be shaped by himself alone. Her physiological changes should have prompted gradual alterations in his own attitude and behavior so that the new course ahead appeared logical. Instead he had been taken by surprise. He could still get where he planned, but the route was altered.

Oscar heard the Nash Rambler come into the garage. Well, more accurately, he heard the automatic garage door open and close. He loved the sound because for two decades at the other house he had had to get out of his car, yank up the door, get back in the

184

car, drive in, get out, close the door behind him. Now it was all done with two pushes on two buttons-- progress there, at least! But what was Curtis doing home?

He found his son spread along the family room couch, the Zenith television warming up across the room. "I thought you were with the Bridges this evening, one of your last nights together for the summer."

"I was supposed to be. Made a big mistake."

"Want some advice from an objective observer?"

"I guess so. See, I got a postcard a few days ago from a girl I went out with a few times last year at Westminster. You know, just saying she had a good summer and was looking forward to seeing me in another week."

"You kept it to yourself, of course."

"I meant to, but, without thinking, I used it as a bookmark in *Great Expectations*, which I'd just finished reading for my fall seminar. And, well, Sarah saw it and accused me of wanting only a 'summer romance' with her, a meaningless 'fling.'"

"She's worried you'll forget her once you're back in Fulton. And it does happen a lot with college men. Did you point out how faithful Pip is for all those years, even when Estella is probably just using him?"

Curtis sat up and tossed a pillow to the other end of the couch. "I told her that she was being irrational, that I'd be down lots of weekends. I even said I wouldn't date anyone at Westminster this semester."

"But that didn't help, obviously, as here you are."

"I'm tell you, she got hot, completely out of control. Said I was like 'all the other boys,' whatever that means. Said I might as well go home and start packing my bags so I could be with 'my kind' as quickly as possible." He paused, and Oscar did feel some sympathy. "Did Mom—uh, did women—do that sort of thing on you, go crazy out of nowhere?"

"Well, there's a reason they say that women are fickle. Their emotions, you know, are affected by— well, their bodies. Until they reach a certain age, they blow hot and cold, change their minds, go ballistic at the silliest things. Sarah will calm down. Give her a day or so."

"I don't have a day or so. Tomorrow starts my last week of work, then I need to be on campus for fall registration the following Monday. Sarah says her parents have decided to make a sudden trip out to California to see her aunt, who's been sick. I'm sure she could stay here if she wanted to. She could keep working at the Turntable and start classes while they're away."

What Oscar would like was for this unconventional Sarah to break off their 'romance,' summer or otherwise. He believed more appropriate relationships would develop with students from similar Missouri backgrounds. This summer would turn out to have been a brief detour, if a pleasant one, on the road to a predictable, stable life, a life a lot like his own.

As the theme song for *My Favorite Martian* filled the family room, Oscar wondered if his desire to direct *Come Back, Little Sheba* with Marsha Baudin would--or already had--detoured him from the path he'd committed to many years ago.

# Chapter Twenty-five: Fires

On Wednesday, Marsha Baudin came to Oscar's office. "Have you a minute?" she asked softly, glancing back over her shoulder as if, it seemed to him, they were already involved in a conspiracy. A bit more loudly she added, "I have some ideas about the fall schedule for drama."

"Um, of course. The play." He pointed to the chair on the other side of his desk, trying not to notice how youthful and fit she looked in a bright sundress with exposed shoulders.

She pulled the chair toward the wall, more out of any passerby's line of sight. At least she had left the door open, though slightly. She went back to her subdued voice. "*Little Sheba*? No. No, about the other night—"

"You're okay? You certainly look better than—when I saw you last."

She leaned forward and spoke barely above a whisper. "I feel I owe you an explanation, more than I said at the time. What happened has nothing to do with you." She straightened up, squared her shoulders, took a deep breath, and continued softly. "Where to begin—"

Oscar decided it was best to say as little possible. He had given her a lift, simple as that. (Of course, if it had really been so simple, why the story about jumping Roger's truck?)

"Before I came here, I was running a community program in Kansas City, three neighborhood theaters in different areas, funded by the city and private contributions. It was a good job, what I'd trained for."

"Um-hm. KC's a nice city."

"I would have stayed there, but, well, I met this man, a very successful eye surgeon. He liked to act and was a major donor. We got to know each other. A bit too well, I guess, as he's married." She leaned back in the chair and crossed her legs.

"Ah."

"Anyway, we had to end it, and that's when I applied here, making, I thought, a clean break. I've always wondered if I should teach one day, so maybe this was providential. You had the new program, after all, which looked promising. It would be a fresh start."

"But—?"

"Yeah, but." Another deep breath. "After I'd accepted the position and given notice to my landlord, my 'friend' called, said the fire was still burning. He claimed he would get a divorce."

"I'm sorry, but are you sure I need to know all this? It's private, between you two—well, or the three of you." He meant the man's wife.

"Please, I feel I need to be honest with you. I thought that chapter of my life was over, and I went to tell him that, to make it final. But he was so convincing, so—well, charming that I believed his—lies. It turns out he just wanted one more fling."

"That's bad, but you're free now, right? And the university is really behind this theater initiative. You've made a new start. Well, maybe you're even coming back to a plan that had been in the back of your mind for a long time--that is, becoming a teacher."

"Yes. The relationship has been over for a several months. But you see, I didn't leave him completely behind—or something of his came with me."

Oscar's eyes widened. Again, he resolved to say little.

"I'd been taking that new medication, one that interrupts a woman's natural—cycle." She made a stern face. "What happened wasn't supposed to happen."

Oscar didn't know what she was talking about--a drug? He thought her story an old one.

"I knew I couldn't stay at the university here, unmarried and in—in my condition, so I made arrangements." She wiped her eyes with a Kleenex she'd pulled from her dress pocket. "This is so hard. You see, I'm Catholic. What I did was against God's laws as well as the state's. But I didn't know what else to do. A friend knew someone who knew someone in Chicago."

"Ah."

"The—uh, procedure was worse than I anticipated. I guess it always is. Anyway, that's why I needed your help, I was exhausted." A grimace. "But you've been so supportive of me and the program, you have a right to know. Without you, I don't know what I would have done."

"Really, anyone would have helped." How he wished Mid had come with him that night! (And where the hell *had* she been that night?)

Marsha leaned forward again, uncrossing her legs. "I'm afraid I've made you an ally, asking you keep my secret. No one--no one in Fairfield but you knows the truth about me."

Oscar assured her he would not mention her past to a soul. Nor would what he knew affect his relationship with her in any way. He was a senior faculty member; she was a junior colleague. She was in charge of theater production; he would direct *Come Back, Little Sheba*. The topic never needed to come up again.

When she had been gone for an hour, he walked to the library, wondering. Surely she had friends she could have called--the person "who knew someone who knew someone," for instance. And where the heck was her family in all this? Couldn't she have gone back to them? Especially now that her condition was—resolved—all the fires were out.

In the library he learned about Enovid, the first drug approved by the FDA as an oral contraceptive.

Millions of couples had begun to use the pill in the early 1960s, and a Connecticut law prohibiting sale of the pill had been struck down by the Supreme Court. Though abortion remained illegal, it was clear today's women were significantly more able to control when they would have children than their mothers had been.

Oscar knew that Mid kept up on medical issues, but she'd never talked about this with him. After Carol's birth, her doctor told her it was highly unlikely she'd ever be pregnant again. But this was important information for their children. He resolved to bring it up, but in a way that wouldn't suggest why he was suddenly interested.

He saw his opportunity several nights later. After dinner he asked, "Have you heard how Ellie is doing with Jack gone?" It was unusually cool that evening, and he'd suggested they take their coffee out to the patio. Oscar knew this was unusual, as he generally retreated to the television or his study; but from here he could nod up the hill in the direction of the Newton house.

"She seems surprisingly content. They weren't doing anything together, just occupying the same house. I think she's moving on."

"After—how many years was it?"

"I don't think that matters. It's the situation right now. Ah, there's my little friend, the wren. See him?"

She loved the wren's loud call, "teakettle-teakettle-teakettle." With it the male tries to lure a female to the nest he's building. And this one had found that the supports under their fiberglass patio roof made a perfect place to set up housekeeping.

"Yes. He's got all he needs except the girl. Hmm. You don't suppose Jack Newton has, um, other interests? The infamous 'other woman.'"

"Nobody has said anything to me. And you know what gossips we women are, especially those who play bridge."

He set his coffee cup down and began to light his pipe, a stalling technique he routinely called on when necessary. "Well, you know what I was reading the other day? All about this new birth control method, 'The Pill.' I guess you know all about that."

"Yes." She switched her attention from the wren, singing to the neighborhood, to Oscar in his deck chair. "Is there a special reason you were reading up on this topic?"

"Oh, some of us were talking in the building the other day about how this is going to encourage a lot of extra-marital affairs, if, you know, women aren't worried about ending up — 'with child.'"

"So, married men like Jack can fool around with other women--married women, younger women, any women--and not worry about the consequences? And you think women are eager to jump into bed with an attractive man because they know they won't get knocked up? It's the end of monogamy as we know it!"

"Sure. I mean, isn't that why men have always had to be cautious, wait until marriage and all?"

She looked back at her wren, sending out his call. "And women, in your view, withhold their favors until they've locked their man in holy matrimony, which guarantees them security for the rest of their life? Are you sure there are no other reasons for women not to sleep with men whenever they feel like it?"

Oscar tamped down his pipe but suspected he'd started another fire—or two. "I don't know. I was just taken by surprise with this--the battle of the sexes enters a new phase."

# Chapter Twenty-six: Paces

Oscar was not happy when he heard that Roger Stone would be the pitcher for Team A. It was likely his student was as good at that as any other sport. Oscar wouldn't want Roger to go easy on him when he came up to bat; but he would really like to tag one this year. Irrationally, he believed such a feat would resolve his current worries.

Around 4:00, cars began to pull up the Millers' drive, park in front of the barn, and disgorge men with baseball gloves, women and picnic baskets, children holding their plastic toys. By 5:00 many would be sitting out on lawn chairs and talking about summer vacations.

"I finished *The Princess of Mars* the day you gave it to me," Roger said to Oscar as they walked toward the field in back of the barn. The red building provided a backdrop behind home plate, with the sheep herded into a pen on the other side. "Monday morning at 8:00 I was at the library to get the next two books. The property of liquids never entered my head as I dodged the radium bullets of green men, hid from white apes, rode flyers beneath the moons of Mars."

"I thought you'd like the books. Burroughs could write well, but what he could really do is tell an adventure story. And they're not bad when read a second or a third time."

"There's also the love element. Who wouldn't want to win Dejah Thoris? But, the funniest thing is, on Thursday morning I had a breakthrough on the dissertation. I went to sleep freezing in the polar regions of Barsoom and woke up in the middle of a simple but elegant path through the labyrinth of my earthly calculations."

"Just as the doctor predicted. Let me know when you want me to look it over. Ah, the captains are getting ready to throw the bat to see who goes first. I guess I'll have to break off communication for the next hour or so."

"You *are* the enemy," laughed Roger.

Without anyone's engineering it, a gentleman's set of rules had taken shape for this friendly annual competition. The pitchers were careful to lob the ball to the few women who wanted to play and to the older men. Any younger man, though, might be confronted with the rising fastball, the breaking curve, the elusive slider.

Each side had an accomplished catcher, who wore a mask and a chest protector. Arthur James' quick magician hands would be catching Roger today; and Harold Miller, Team B's captain, put on the gear for Oscar's team. Harold had not said who was pitching, but hinted that he'd recruited a new player who might make an impact.

"Here comes their star," acknowledged Arthur, pointing to a red Mustang leaving a trail of dust in the driveway and pulling up to the barn. "Just in time to take the field."

"Who's that?" asked Roger, "a new graduate student? I don't recognize the car."

"That's Dr. Miller's guest, Marsha Baudin, from Theater," explained Arthur." I learned she played softball at college and invited her to join us. Harold and I flipped a coin to see who got her." They watched the slender young woman jump out and start jogging toward them.

"What position did she play?" asked Oscar casually. He most often was at first base.

"Pitcher," said Arthur, leaning forward. "And, observing her general form, I have a feeling her pitching form is going to be pretty good." Arthur curled his index finger around to his thumb and held it up like a lens to zero in on the cut-off jeans and Kansas Jayhawk jersey.

Dr. Miller pointed out, "Mr. Stone has great pitching and hitting form, but a mighty big strike zone. We plan to take away your offensive power." He waved to Marsha.

Arthur grinned. "I don't know if Professor Baudin can hit, but I plan to study her strike zone very carefully. Let's see, it's above the knees and — what? mid-, um, -chest?"

"Good Lord, Arthur! Just send up your leadoff hitter. Team B, take your places."

Marsha had her glove open as she came up to Harold, who dropped the softball into the pocket. "Do you need to throw any warm-up pitches?" he asked.

"Just a few. Hi, everyone. Sorry I'm late."

There were greetings and introductions. Then they trotted out to their positions.

Oscar looked over to where the spectators were gathering. Sure enough, there was Mid unfolding a lawn chair beside their neighbor Ellie Newton and her good friend Charlotte, all three already in deep conversation. He hadn't been sure how to take it earlier when Mid told him to go easy and avoid injury to his musician's fingers.

He saw Roger standing by the corner of the barn, one long arm angled up to rest on a fence post. Oscar wondered if his student was remembering what he'd said about coming to Martha's rescue. But Roger may have already forgotten and was just studying a fellow athlete.

The former college player was not lobbing in soft pitches, but going with the full windmill windup. Oscar could see the ball rise, curve, dip; but it still didn't appear she was giving it all she could. He hoped she'd been coached on how to handle different players.

He was impressed that his department chair was catching her pitches neatly. Low inside, high outside, right down the middle. Then it occurred to Oscar that Harold was not responsible for what was happening.

Marsha Baudin was hitting his mitt wherever he held it--*smack*!

Harold threw the next pitch to the third baseman. "Around the horn," he called. And the infield caught and threw the ball in the established order, with Oscar sending it back to Marsha.

"What's the rule on stealing bases?" she asked him.

"We don't. It's mostly, let 'em hit, see if we can make more runs."

"Good." She winked. "I have a mean pick-off pitch, anyway." And the game began.

With her on the mound, this innocent afternoon of play was looking more complicated than Oscar had anticipated. And it came at a time when he longed for a simple contest, with men at play in a familiar context.

Oscar decided on his strategy: stay within the moment. He would take the throws from his infielders and get runners out at first; swing for the hit that was right in each situation, not go for a home run. (And don't think, he cautioned, about whether Mid was watching alongside Marsha, hearing Ellie talk about the end of a marriage, or getting campus gossip from Charlotte.) And he did well until the second time he came to bat.

"Big stick at the plate, infield," Marsha called to the opposition when Oscar stepped to the plate. He'd flown out deep to left his first time up. "Better move the fielders back." With runners on first and third,

Oscar was expected to bring home the runs in what could prove their best chance of the day.

On the mound Roger had the same relaxed, confident look on his face Oscar had seen when he was playing basketball: an exceptional man who knew he could do what he wanted when he wanted with ordinary people. Oscar should not try for too much. Protect the plate, make contact.

But when Roger whipped successive fastballs past him, Oscar's competitive nature kicked in. He tapped the bat in the middle of the plate, smiled at his opponent, and dug in for the next pitch. He concluded that Roger, infected by the warrior spirit of John Carter, would try to get him on three consecutive fastballs. So he started his swing early, confident he now knew the pace of Roger's windmill delivery and the rise on his fastball.

As his bat whistled over the plate, Oscar realized the ball was still several yards out in front of him, floating gently toward him like a balloon. It was a beautifully disguised change-of-pace. The sound of the ball landing softly in Arthur James' mitt came just after Oscar's bat wrapped around his back, wrenching his shoulder.

"Stri-iiike three!" announced Arthur James and then fired the ball out to third base. "Around the horn!"

Oscar managed to turn his grunt of effort into a compliment. "Oh, ho-ho! You got me on that one," and trotted back to the barn. "Why didn't one of you tell me about his change-up?" he joked, picking up his glove. He played on despite soreness in his shoulder.

He later regained some stature--though at a cost--when he rushed a bunt by his rival, Arthur James, down the first base line. With a flap of the glove, he waved off the pitcher, who was also charging, fielded the ball with his bare hand, and, spinning, threw to the second baseman covering the bag.

"Out at first," called Dr. Miller.

"Slick play there, Professor," admitted Arthur, huffing from the exertion.

Marsha had ended up right next to Oscar. As they started to walk out to their positions, she, presumably falling back into her identity as college athlete, gave him an openhanded swat on his rear end and said softly, "Nice pick-up." The sound of that slap--*smack!*--seemed to Oscar as loud as a sonic boom, ricocheting off the barn and racing past the spectators, across the town, out into the land.

# Chapter Twenty-seven: Parts

"Cheeky girl," observed Mid as they drove home. "She acts like she's been in Fairfield for decades and is best friends with everyone."

"Professor Baudin? You're exaggerating." But Marsha did seem to turn on the charm during the meal, moving between groups and chattering away about campus and local events.

"Yes, your theater chum."

He tapped the temperature gauge on the Jag's dash, as if there might be a problem there. "We're not pals." Oscar admitted to himself, though, that an actress would know how to play the role of social butterfly, pretending to more intimate relations than existed in fact.

"But you're going to be working together, right?"

"Actually, she will have almost nothing to do with *Little Sheba*. She'll start lobbying different offices for money and working with other departments, like art and English, whose students can contribute. She also wants to establish connections with local officials so this can be a community effort, not just a university one."

Mid huffed. "Well, she seemed mighty familiar for a junior faculty member. She had Arthur eating out of her hand." Marsha and Oscar's colleague had been with the Millers and Ellie at the table next to Oscar and Mid's. Arthur had jumped up to get her a drink, recommend desserts, fill her in on who was who.

"Arthur will eat out of the hand of any attractive woman, even yours."

He could see her turn toward him. "You think so? *Even* me?"

Oscar tried to think of a way to change the topic. "This is Curtis' last week on the job, isn't it?"

"Yes. And something has happened between him and Sarah. Has he talked to you?"

"He got a card from a girl at Westminster, perfectly innocent. Apparently, though, she took it as an insult to her."

"She's a talented girl, but I won't be unhappy when our boy is back in Fulton." Oscar agreed, almost adding that he would be "with his own kind." But then he suspected that might not sound right in the changing climate of the times.

"He's been asking me all summer to ride with him one day on his well-finding job. I guess it had better be this week since classes do start Thursday. If he has girl troubles, that will give him the opportunity to get sage advice." Did Oscar dare say he could do with some suggestions himself about how to deal with females?

"Wednesday might be good. Ellie has asked me to go into St. Louis with her. Shopping and—seeing an old friend."

"Oh? You going to go?"

Oscar and Mid seldom traveled separately, even on day trips, unless the faculty wives' club scheduled an event.

"I think she also wants to talk. There's a lot to work through when a marriage breaks up after twenty-five years."

How true, thought Oscar, pulling into the driveway and pushing the remote for the garage door. There's even plenty to think through when a marriage continues after twenty-five years! Right now he wanted to escape all such considerations and retreat to the world of Edgar Rice Burroughs—or a fantasy of his own making—or a remembered/idealized game of baseball.

He reviewed today's contest in his mind. Team B had won a narrow victory, more because they had some lucky breaks than that they were better players. Marsha's pitching was as good as Roger's, and she received a lot of the credit from both sides. He winced when he recalled her impromptu slap on his behind, a complete break from the expected.

Maybe, he thought, that what was attractive to Carol about being in the Army during peacetime: everyone is given clear assignments; you're all on the same team; the surprises in training exercises cause no permanent harm. Somebody does have to study and identify the big picture. But the individual soldier is given tasks, trains to perform them, and learns to ignore the distractions that might complicate the mission. Perhaps Mid found a similar simplicity with mechanical clocks. If all the pieces are sound and in the right place, time is kept.

Mid stopped in the utility room and was inspecting the cuckoo parts. Pausing at the doorway to the kitchen, Oscar asked, "How's that coming?"

"I think I'm close. It's run for short periods, but then conked out. Still, the bird comes out when the minute hand passes 12:00 and chirps the right number of hours."

"That's good. By the way, my horn is making nice sounds as well. Now all I need is a little group to play with, a jazz combo, for instance."

He passed on into the kitchen and headed toward his study. The organized world of music appealed to him tonight: the regularity of keys, the principle of octaves, the regular time signatures. Within those structures, good musicians could improvise, composing a tune and working through variations. Everything fit within a system and reached a final harmony. He considered adherence to form a virtue in art and science.

Literary composition should be similar. When he had been writing for radio in college, he felt an enormous satisfaction at a completed script. And he was often praised for being able to adapt roles for specific actors or adjust to technical limitations even at the last minute. He had absorbed the structure of radio drama from years of listening to such fine shows as Orson Welles' *War of the Worlds* and Dorothy L. Sayers' *The Man Born to Be King*, which was broadcast in a dozen episodes.

He also loved comedies and the better soap operas, which had to be especially scripted to end on a suspenseful note but also draw listeners forward in the broad arc of the story. For parties, he had sometimes parodied popular shows, using college personalities and campus buildings to poke fun at current events.

Oscar felt an affinity for William Inge, the author of the play, *Come Back, Little Sheba*. Both men had been born and raised in Kansas and both taught at Missouri colleges. Inge was recognized for his understanding of the American Midwest in his portrayal of small-town life. He was, though, an alcoholic, and many of his characters suffer from emotional frustration, often caused by confining sexual mores.

Had Oscar just been successful over the years in repressing his own desires, driving himself to fulfill expectations established by others? His mother, a strict disciplinarian, had insisted he apply himself in school and rise above the level of his carpenter father to status in a profession. He'd left home after college to escape her control, but now it occurred to him he might have internalized her vision of himself without realizing it.

Inge had the good fortune to meet Tennessee Williams in St. Louis, who encouraged him in his writing career. Oscar had been told by several of his professors at Salinas Wesleyan that he should pursue his literary gifts. Had he made a wrong turn when he decided to go on in science? If, after college, he'd traveled from Salinas to St. Louis rather than Jefferson City, would his abilities have been channeled in another direction?

He took his saxophone out and began to improvise. In his head he heard characters from *Little Sheba* expressing their sorrows and their dreams in music. Lola was washing dishes at the tiny sink in her tiny kitchen. "*I used to wear pretty dresses,*" she sang, "*And throw the boys my kisses. / Where are the beaus I used to know, / Where did the good times go?*"

Doc would be drinking coffee at the table, close enough to Lola he could reach out and touch her. But he wouldn't hear her voice as he gazed into the dark cup. "*Do not think of the past, my men; / Finish the tasks for today. / Youth is a waste, my friend, / Hard work is the only way.*"

What would Inge say himself? That was one of the advantages and disadvantages of being an author: characters could speak for you, but your audience doesn't always know which voices your truth.

"What are you playing?" Mid asked. She was standing in the doorway. "It's mournful."

"Oh, I'm just fooling around, daydreaming in music almost."

"Well, I'm going to bed. Come when you're ready."

When had it happened that their bedtimes were different? For years, they reserved that part of the day for their most intimate talks. Of course, now and then he was up late getting ready for class. And, even in the summer, an idea for his research might him keep him in the study an extra half hour or hour. But at some point, a corner had been turned, and going to bed at different times became the norm. Was he, then, stopping in his study tonight when he didn't have to? Or was Mid hurrying to get into bed before he would join her?

# Chapter Twenty-eight:
# Chairs

In addition to the usual students dropping by his office on Monday to talk about classes, Oscar had three visitors, each one adding to his general anxiety.

"Oscar," Harold Miller asked, "when you have a minute, will you drop by the office?"

"Sure. This afternoon?" Probably the standard university politics, Oscar concluded--who gets extra money, positions, resources. The school year always starts with such negotiation. Oscar gave good advice but, citing the time-consuming nature of his research, begged off direct involvement. Was he going to be pulled in this year?

"Any time between 2:00 and 4:00." Then as Harold turned to go, he added, "Nice game Sunday. We have a good group in the department these days. The future looks bright."

At the picnic there had been talk about where their graduate program was headed. Senior faculty needed to raise more grant money, and the theorists were being outpaced by the experimentalists. Both government and corporate sponsors wanted measurable results, clear application to industry and progress. But it was much harder for theorists to show

how new models of what went on inside an atom or outside the galaxy would make America more competitive and more prosperous. The theories behind nuclear energy and nuclear bombs were established; what was wanted in the mid-1960s was application.

Arthur James was having success with new waterjet technology, building more and more powerful systems to drive a huge volume of water through tiny orifices; the resulting streams could cut timber, stone, metal. Oscar teased him that he was still playing with the water pistols of his childhood, but Arthur was getting inquires about the latest models. Cooperative contracts with industry were being drawn up.

Oscar was sure Arthur's understanding of the physics involved was rudimentary, as he was known to leave the research and calculations to his graduate assistants. But he was a slick salesman and could probably sell miniature waterjets to gullible homeowners, especially women. When had the world of science been turned over to businessmen?

Oscar shared his unhappiness at the profession's decline with his star theorist who came in to leave the latest section of the dissertation. "I sometimes wonder if I should have gone into industry," Oscar mused. "I would have been rich by now, ready to retire to the Virgin Islands."

"I don't know," said Roger. "Success in business might be like the Valley of Dor, from which there is no escape. Well, no escape for anyone but John Carter."

"You mean a lifestyle of luxury is hard to give up, entrapping the successful?"

"Something like that." Roger shifted his long body in the straight back chair across from Oscar. "Listen, I had a—um, rather strange conversation with Marsha Baudin in the library this morning."

"Oh?" Oscar thumbed through the handwritten pages Roger had given him.

"Yeah, first she talked sports with me, the ball game. But then she seemed to want to know all about you--your wife, if you have children, how long you've been here, if you're interested in moving on."

"That's really none of her business. I trust you kept your answers succinct."

"To be sure, especially considering how she—how you had done her a favor."

Oscar regretted again the night he'd answered her phone call—and lied to Mid about where he's been. His life had veered off on a strange path toward an end he couldn't see. "Being new," he suggested to Roger, "she's probably curious about everyone, even the strikeout king."

"Hey, that was just one at bat, and I got a bit carried away in the heat of the moment. But it was a good game, and I can say this: that Baudin, she's a good athlete, very—fit."

"Yes, strong arm, and she steps into her pitch." Oscar had had a good view from first base of her long legs. In an effort to appear transparent, he added, "I can't remember if I told you, but I've offered to direct a play on campus this fall, helping out the new theater program. I'll coordinate with Professor Baudin, but as program director, she'll be off establishing connections, support, that sort of thing. She may have just wanted to hear that I'm a reliable colleague."

When the phone buzzed for Oscar, Roger waved and stepped out. Mid confirmed that she was going to St. Louis with Ellie on Wednesday and encouraged Oscar to plan to take the day with Curtis. He agreed it would be good for both of them.

The next knock on his door was Marsha's. "Got a minute?"

He hoped his face didn't reveal what he thought. "Uh, yes, but just for a sec. The chair wants to see me about—oh, the usual stuff."

"I'm going to have learn about that *usual stuff*. I've been a student and a graduate student; now I need to start thinking like a faculty member."

"It's a strange world, academia."

"I suppose so." She settled herself in the same chair Roger had sat in. "Everyone at the picnic seemed pretty normal, though. Well, not Professor James. He belongs in the world of theater, with his jokes and sleight of hand."

"He is tricky. You may want to keep your distance."

"Oh, I know his type--flashy, but not to be trusted. I'm looking for the steady, what-you-see-is-what-you-get kind of man. Someone like you, for instance." She crossed her legs and leaned back in the chair. "Anyway, that's not what I wanted to ask about: who in the Chancellor's office might have been involved in theater in the past. I need some contacts."

"To tell you the truth, I don't have the slightest idea. I try to keep out of personalities. The world of physics is objective, impersonal, even cold."

She raised her eyebrows. "And I was so sure thermodynamics involved heat."

"Now that I think about it, Professor James might be the one to help you. He knows everyone, and you understand how to—well, deal with him. Look, sorry to rush you, but—"

She jumped up. "Of course. And I can come back if I have more questions. I see your office hours posted on the door. Or we could meet for coffee downtown one day."

Oscar made a show of rising and filing Roger's papers in a file cabinet, though he put it in a folder labeled "Projectile Properties."

It was a bit before 2:00, but he walked directly to Harold's office and was grateful to see Marsha heading for the building's side exit. A talk about funding priorities with a colleague seemed more attractive now than it had in the morning.

"Oscar, come in," Harold said, gesturing to a pair of captain's chairs he had set up by a small table in front of the window. "I've got several things to discuss."

"That's why I love the summer," sighed Oscar, sitting. "From mid-June to early September, I just think, read, and write. Classes begin, and life gets complicated."

"So true. But first, the good news: I've had a number of calls over the summer concerning your latest paper on equilibrium properties of liquids. It's good news for the university, a prestigious article in a prestigious journal. People are noticing."

"I tend to forget about past projects when I'm in the middle of a new one. And the time it takes for things to get into print means one's ideas are out of sync with the larger community."

"So, there's more to come on this? Good. It puts you in a position to hear what I have to say." He placed his hands on the table. "You know I've been thinking of stepping down as department chair. After a certain number of years, you lose your effectiveness."

Oscar immediately ran through a list of his senior colleagues who might take Harold's place. Anyone but Arthur James!

"Do you know who I think would do a good job in this office? He's already sitting here with me."

"Me?" Oscar had never sought a role in college administration. "You know I have low tolerance for meetings, budget matters, record keeping."

"It's good to get someone who doesn't want the position to take it on. He'll work to help the department, not his own career. As I was saying this

214

morning, we have a strong faculty right now; but we need a new leader. And, of course, there's a nice boost in salary that stays with you in the retirement system."

"Surely, there's a better candidate—"

"You don't have to say anything today. Take some time, talk it over with Mid. You're established, Oscar. You can use your reputation to ensure that the kind of work you believe in gets the recognition it deserves. I don't have to tell you that things are changing in the profession. You can help steer this department, even the university, in the right direction."

Given his children's changing plans, Mid's increasing dissatisfaction with him, and his own uncertainties, Oscar wondered if he could steer himself in the right direction.

# Chapter Twenty-nine: Springs

"Ever seen Boiling Spring?" Curtis asked as they crossed a new section of I-44, formerly Route 66, and headed north on a county road.

"No. It's your mother who likes to see the sights."

"Well, if we can get the well on the old Chapman place," he flipped a slip of paper over to his dad, "in the next fifteen minutes, we might have time to swing by there. It's worth seeing."

Curtis was working the week in Pulaski County, close to Fairfield. So, rather than stay nights at a local motel, he drove home at the end of the day. His dad could ride along and see what he'd been doing all summer. The slip of paper gave the date of drilling and location--"the Chapman farm north of Union." Curtis had gotten more information at the Post Office.

Oscar said, "I've seen Maramec Springs, as you remember."

One summer Mid had insisted the family visit this local attraction. Oscar then used that one occasion to decline trips to other famous Missouri springs. He'd done the same with caves after Onondaga. He repeated to Curtis what he said about both geographical wonders: "I suspect they're all the same."

"Yeah. What I like about Boiling Spring is that you don't know what you're looking at when you first see it. The water comes up in the Gasconade River, stirring an area close to the bank. So you tend to think it's just the river going over rocks or the current swirling."

"Um-hum."

"But the spring is throwing out as much as 80 gallons of water a day, so it's really two streams in one. There can be gravel churning around that's not from the river bottom, but coming from deep underground."

"Um-hum."

"Divers have gone as far as 175 feet down and traced the water back over 1500. There''s a lot going on under the surface and away from where the water boils up; but most people only know there's bubbling in the river."

"Um-hum"

Curtis left the blacktop for a gravel road. "I'm going to warn you," he said, "because time is a factor in recording data, I am about to navigate these back roads in an, um, efficient way."

"Makes sense to me. It's the barometric pressure, right?" Even as he said it, though, Oscar had to grab the armrest on his door. Curtis had taken a curve on a gravel road so fast that Oscar almost fell across the seat.

"Yes. Once I've set the altimeter at a known elevation, I have to be back at the same or another known elevation in an hour to calculate the drift accurately. Air pressure doesn't usually go up *and* down in an hour, so I can use the math I learned in college to adjust readings within that hour--elevation 2 over elevation 1 equals correction factor."

"Ah, my money well spent at Westminster."

Curtis suddenly put on the brakes and slid to a stop, glancing in the rear view mirror. "Wait a minute. Missed a turn."

He cranked the wheels hard to the left, slammed the gears into reverse, popped the clutch, and the car spun backwards. The front wheels barely stayed out of the ditch on the right, the back tires came into the center of the road. He cranked the steering wheel right, shifted into first, gunned the engine, and they shot back the way they had come.

Curtis chuckled. "I hadn't thought about it until recently, but I have been an expense to you, whereas Carol is already earning money. Later, if she goes to college, the GI Bill will pay."

"That's if she stays in." Oscar continued to foresee her shortening her time. At the moment he was also thinking about how his son was "navigating."

Oscar had always prided himself on his driving. He was not reckless, but he bought good cars in order to take highway curves without slowing down, pass slower vehicles cleanly, use power and maneuverability to avoid dangerous situations. The one accident he'd had in his life was not his fault; the driver behind him had fallen asleep.

Part of the reason he enjoyed handling a fine machine had to do with not being able to afford his own until he married. Mid, in fact, had a car before the war; after that it was difficult to purchase one. Her Plymouth became Oscar's first automobile as, in his mind, men generally did the driving. It hadn't occurred to him that his son would become such a skilled driver.

Curtis turned up a lane toward an old farmhouse. "Oh, Carol loves the military. She's excited about her advanced training, which is going to involve espionage techniques."

"You've talked to her recently?"

"Yeah, last weekend, while you were at the picnic. I think we're related to a future Army general." He glanced at the topographical map--folded to show the area he needed to see--which he'd set on the dash. "Okay, coming to what I hope is the Chapman farm."

Oscar stayed in the car as Curtis went up to the porch and talked with an older man in overalls and a worn St. Louis Cardinals cap. Then the two stepped off the porch and walked over to a small structure of concrete blocks, which Oscar assumed was the well house. Curtis took an elevation reading on his altimeter, shook hands with the man, came back to the car.

"Okay. We've got it." He put an X on the topographical map and glanced at his watch. "We've got time to see the spring."

Oscar nodded toward the house. "Do people like that understand why you're snooping around their property? I'd think one of these days you'd been greeted by a shotgun."

"Some are suspicious; but I must have an open face, and most are quite cooperative." He slid around a curve on the loose gravel. "Mr. Chapman back there understood right away that the information about his well--how deep, what layers of rock the driller had to go through, that sort of thing--would help us map what's underground in this area. It'll be good for other folks who want to build a house or drill a new well to know what they have to go through--literally."

"That's not the stereotype of the Ozark hillbilly, then. Of course, what is the stereotype, the Beverly Hillbillies or Li'l Abner?"

"As with Boiling Spring, there's more than meets the eye with these rural folk. By the way, did you know Mom has Mrs. Miller's cuckoo clock chiming?"

"No. When did that happen?"

"Yesterday or the day before. And she thinks she's figured out what the old Lacy clock needs. If she gets that running, she'll be ready to go into business."

"You mean clock repair and restoration? Oh, I don't think she wants to go that far; it's just a hobby. Setting up a business involves paperwork, keeping

220

accounts, understanding taxes. She prefers reading and knitting."

"Well, that's not what she told me. She's looked into having business cards printed and is going to meet with Mr. Agee. He's agreed to supply her with a list of his old customers and some tips on where to get parts. I have a feeling he's enjoying Mom taking an interest in clocks."

"Women! Who can predict what they'll do? Speaking of the species, how is Sarah about your returning to Westminster? She get over seeing the postcard from your friend?"

Curtis chuckled. "Did she! She's decided that's where a basically ordinary guy like me belongs, at a small Midwestern college with others just like me."

"Ah, so you're not good enough for her."

"That seems to be the case." He picked up the map and glanced down the road. "Need to watch for a lane up ahead, on the right."

Oscar turned to look, and Curtis continued. "You know, earlier this summer Mom worried I might just be having fun with Sarah, a typical summer romance in which a young, innocent high school girl gets hurt by the older, college guy. It turned out the other way around."

"Ah. I'm sorry."

"Have to face facts. I guess I'm not really that ambitious—or at least not so sure of myself that I'm ready for the big time. I don't know how people like her have that confidence."

"Don't underestimate yourself. A lot of us take some time to find what we want to do, what we're really capable of. If you jump right in at eighteen and chart your whole life out, it's possible you'll find yourself at forty wondering what in the world you're doing."

The lane ended at the bank of the Gasconade. They got out and looked at the churning water. "It's up today," observed Curtis.

"A lot going on under the surface," Oscar agreed.

He could see small brown pebbles rolling in the water, either coming up from the bottom of the river or perhaps being carried from some underground location miles away and now merging with surface water on a long journey toward the sea.

# Chapter Thirty: Pages

When Oscar heard from Roger that Marsha Baudin had decamped, he felt a profound sense of relief. Unfortunately, it didn't last.

"What do you mean?" he asked his student about Marsha. "She's gone?"

"Left the university, left town, departed. According to what I heard, some older man from her past came in, swooped her up, and the two went off to follow new dreams together."

"It's possible another university made her an offer and that that man was a friend or a relative come to help."

"I think it's strictly a romantic thing. They'd had some sort of affair back in KC, broke it off, but apparently he found he couldn't live without her."

Oscar had trouble taking this in. "And she's resigned her position? After all the work that was done to get her here? Wasn't there even some additional money thrown in for the program?"

"You'd know more about that than I do. All I have is from a faculty member in the drama department who plays basketball with me on Sundays. He says everyone's furious, but she's returning no calls."

"Hmm. Well, I don't know what this will mean about my directing *Little Sheba*, but I suspect someone in that department, or a dean, will be in touch." He took a folder from his desk. "Meanwhile, here's your new material. It's brilliant. You may be over the hill with this."

"More has been churning up from the depths of my calculating mind since I turned that in. Here's the next installment." He passed over a packet of papers.

"No need for John Carter, then?"

"I'm not sure about that, so I've gotten all the Edgar Rice Burroughs Tarzan books I can find from the library. They're page-turners just like the Mars books. So I go from mathematics to fantasy and back again--seems to create a nice balance."

Oscar thought for a minute. "Speaking of balance, what would you think of me going into administration? Still teaching some, of course, but also taking on matters of budget, curriculum, personnel. It would give a bit of variety to my professional life."

Roger leafed through the pages Oscar had turned back. "You'd be good at it, but—"

"But?"

"Oscar, you've got the best mind in the department. If you get pulled into the bureaucratic side of academic life, there won't be anyone left on this faculty who can do what you. Theoretical physicists are rare birds. We don't want them to become extinct."

"That's honest advice, and I appreciate it." He leaned back in his chair. "I've had some people talk to me about possibilities--here and elsewhere--but nothing's definite." He paused. "I am sort of mid-career and should at least look at all my options."

Roger rose and turned to go. "Just don't let some dean from M.I.T. or CalTech dazzle you with an offer to fulfill your dreams!"

Oscar chuckled and waved goodbye.

Later that afternoon he told Mid about the "sky well" that had been built for the now defunct resort on the bluff above Boiling Spring. He'd gotten so busy with the first days of classes and Curtis' packing to go back to Westminster that he'd not told Mid about his day as a well-finder. Nor had he asked about Mid's day in St. Louis with Ellie.

"The facility was short lived," he explained, "but the novelty of raising water from the spring by a bucket arrangement struck my fancy."

He had found Mid once again in the utility room, this time inspecting the Lacy clock. "Tell me about it," she said.

"It was built by a man from the plains counties of Missouri, up north, an immigrant carpenter who earned a fortune building silos for grain storage. He retired rich at age 45, about 1927 or so, with a dream to create a vacation place close enough to St. Louis to attract families for the weekend. Feeling he'd been blessed himself, he wanted to offer inexpensive getaways for hardworking, ordinary citizens, the same kind of people he'd hired to work for him."

"Doesn't sound like a bad idea. How was the water hoisted up to the overlook?"

"The same mechanics they use to bring grain to the top of a silo. He just rigged the bucket system for water rather than solid material. It could deliver 50 gallons a minute."

Mid had the back off the Lacy clock and was twisting a knob at the top of the pendulum rod. "See this little wheel? Turn it this way, and it shortens the length of the pendulum spring; the other way increases it."

"Yes, the longer the pendulum, the slower the clock runs. Gravity's a constant, but distance changes. So, you adjust length to keep perfect time--or get it as close as you can."

"And now that I figured out how to maintain the tension on this main arbor—" She pointed into the works. "—I believe it's going to be as reliable as any modern spring-driven clock." She turned the clock around to face her and reached around to nudge the pendulum bob. Oscar could hear the clock start ticking.

"That's very nice. Anyway, the former silo builder turned entrepreneur used the architectural design for his silos to build five little bungalows up on the hill, all constructed of local hardwoods and stone. One had a small restaurant and a store that sold fishing equipment, tubes to float on the river, swimwear, goggles. He offered cottage rentals at a very low price."

"It must have failed if it's not there now." The Lacy clock began to chime--one, two, three, four, five times. Oscar looked at the face: 5:00 o'clock. Mid smiled. "Ah. Now it's on to the cuckoo bird. So, what did in the Gasconade Bluff Resort?"

"Ah, that." He shrugged. "Bad timing."

"Timing? Oh, the Depression?"

"Exactly. He'd sunk his entire fortune into the venture. After it opened the stock market crashed. His four bungalows sat mostly empty for three years. He had funded it all himself, at least, so there were no banks to foreclose; but finally he had to shut down the resort." Oscar looked through the door to the patio. "To me, though, I can't help thinking if he'd tried something like this in the 1950s--or even now--there might have been a Disneyland of the Midwest."

"I think that's pie in the sky, not a sky well."

Oscar sighed. "Maybe I'm just attracted to the idea of a man taking a new direction in life, turning a page over and starting a new story."

Mid pushed back from her worktable. "Well, a trial separation makes sense, then."

"Separation? What are you talking about?"

"You and me. We decide to spend some time apart, evaluate our marriage. You could look into whatever it is you want to do that's not physics--direct plays, write television shows, spend time with—with other people."

"Hey, I was just thinking out loud, wondering about what might have been."

"The way these things work—Ellie and her friend told me all this when we were visiting in St. Louis. The way it works is that one of us moves out for a time--a few months, I guess--and we see if we want to stay together or—you know."

"I *don't* know, but I'm not moving out. Where is this coming from, anyway?"

Mid glanced back at the clock, ticking steadily away. "I guess it would have to be me who moves out. That's probably best, anyway, as I don't think you'd adapt well to a new place. Ellie is interested in the idea I take a room in her house. You've never cooked and don't know much about domestic chores. But you understand where everything is here and you can buy frozen dinners."

"Wait a minute! How did we get to this point?"

"Oh, come now. You don't want to do anything with me any more. You love the idea of a getaway place, but won't even look at lots on Avalon Lake. I explain how interesting these antique clocks are, and you fade out after a few minutes--even though I know there are half a dozen physics principles involved you could tell me about. I make a new friend in Ellie Newton, our neighbor and your colleague's wife-- well, soon-to-be ex-wife--you don't even ask why we've hit it off so well."

Oscar tried to focus. Was she really proposing divorce? They had raised three children. They'd just bought a new house. They had achieved a comfortable way of life with enough income to be saving for retirement. What had he missed? Had there been a day on which she'd told him they were now officially going different directions? Had he been paying so little attention that he'd agreed? If so, how in the world did he back up and cancel that agreement?

# Volume Four: Lake. Chapter Thirty-one: Notes

Oscar threw his script down on the dinette in the family room and growled, "Now the set designer has quit!" He still anticipated Mid's questions about what that meant and what he would have to do to get things right. All he heard was the quiet ticking of the Lacy clock, now established on the sideboard in the front entrance.

Oscar worried that his whole production was in jeopardy. The project had begun auspiciously, with him in great spirits and with all entertaining high hopes. Bill Marks from the theater department had volunteered to take the central role of Doc; and a veteran of the Fairfield community drama group, Melissa Remington, was a perfect Lola. Enough students had come for tryouts to fill out the rest of the small cast, including a bright and attractive co-ed from the chemistry program, Jan Reynolds, who would be Marie.

But planning rehearsals with everyone's different schedules, moderating the temperamental moods of actors, and keeping up with his own teaching had proven more of a challenge than he'd anticipated. Bill showed up with great reliability but said he never felt he had "become" Doc. Melissa had three children who needed her presence at school events, club meetings, and "play dates" (whatever they were!). Thank goodness for Jan, whose only drawback Oscar couldn't complain about: now and then she insisted she had to study for her classes.

It felt like he was juggling chainsaws, and this last development threatened to destroy the whole stage. He almost wished Marsha Baudin were still around so he could ask her what to do do. Or better yet, dump the whole project back on the person who'd gotten him involved in the first place. But the last he'd heard, via campus gossip, was that her lover had finally asked his wife for a divorce and planned to marry Marsha after all. She'd never return to Fairfield.

Increasingly convinced that he had taken a wrong turn--or several wrong turns--somewhere after college, Oscar saw directing a play as an opportunity to establish options for his future. Not that he was resigning his position (though he had put in a formal application to Enchantment College), Oscar felt he was at a turning point. He steadfastly refused to let himself see it as a mid-life crisis that would lead to a red Austin-Healey and a blonde bimbo.

Picking up the script, already worn and smudged with notes he'd scribbled in the margins, he wandered into his study and got out his saxophone. Perhaps music would soothe the irritated director. The little combo he'd recruited for the performance had proven an unexpected boon in his time of trials. The Rockers of Age, a group in their 60s, let him sit in on their jam sessions; and he'd even begun composing songs linked to the plot of *Come Back, Little Sheba. Maybe*

231

*that's what I should have become*, he thought: *an opera composer.*

He envisioned himself acting as dean at Enchantment for three to five years, then being appointed by a grateful president to the post of Artist in Residence--playwright, musician, director. He would enter a second academic career in an entirely different capacity.

The stack of exams to be graded on his desk, however, reminded him that he was for the time being a professor of physics. And not only did he have his usual courses to teach (an introductory lecture class and an advanced theoretical class), but he also had to finish shepherding Roger Stone through his dissertation.

"The real question," his student had told him a few days earlier, "is will I be able to find enough Edgar Rice Burroughs books to last the semester. I've fallen into the Pellucidar series now and wonder if I'll ever reach the surface!"

The amazingly prolific science fiction author invented many worlds, most in outer space; but the land of Pellucidar was inside the earth. Of course, it had Burroughs' usual cast of strange creatures, ancient rites, and human-like beings who needed a savior from the outside. In this case the hero from elsewhere is David Innes, a mining engineer of the present age who inadvertently tunnels into a world described by Burroughs as "At the Earth's Core."

"You'll rise to the occasion," Oscar laughingly told Roger, who had brought two cups of coffee from the dining hall for a review of his progress. "Make a note to yourself and paste it on your bathroom mirror: 'This degree is my meal ticket for the future.'"

"Ah, I do understand that," Roger mused. "But I have begun to wonder what the future holds, especially as I learn more about how political the academic life is. Are you, for instance, still dodging the job as next department chair?"

"It's a challenge. Arthur James, the magician, clearly wants it, and most of my colleagues know he'd be a disaster in that role."

"From what the grad students say, he's more interested in chasing skirts than building the department, though he has bamboozled a number of government agencies into funding his waterjet project. Surely, there's a reasonable alternative you can champion?"

"To tell the truth, I'd kind of like my friend, Dr. Rust, to consider it. He hates administrative work as much as I do, but he'd be fair and do the job." Oscar took a sip of his coffee. "Between you and me, it may be the only way he can get full professor."

"Because he's been sucked into the unified field theory trap?"

Theoretical physicists since Einstein had been intrigued by the possibility of combining principles of relativity and classical physics in one grand design. William Rust was convinced he was on the right track and had abandoned more conventional research in pursuit of this chimerical ideal. But to get that final professorial rank, one needed publications in respected academic journals, not a book manuscript that might--but more likely would not--change the entire field.

"Exactly. And he has daughters getting ready for college. As frugal as he's been, Linda has never worked, and eight years of tuition are going to be a strain." Oscar also had seen signs that Bill was bored with academic work. He had an odd interest in — well, pornography.

"Ah, yes. Another drawback in the life of a faculty member: the pay is never high, and supporting a family is a strain. It's good my love interests are fictional."

"Dian the Beautiful of Amoz?" grinned Oscar.

"She'll do for now, assuming she escapes being eaten by the Mahars."

That species of flying reptiles in Pellucidar is female, able to reproduce without the involvement of males. The Mahars "Great Secret" of their pathogenesis is carefully guarded.

Oscar was beginning to see how women might want to live in a world they could control. Ellie Newton was getting along fine without her husband, thanks in part to Mid and other married women who'd rallied behind someone they felt had been wronged. While some in the next generation--like Louis' Suzanne--seemed comfortable with the traditional role of wife and mother, others were rejecting traditional roles and demanding all the rights of men.

Oscar's own daughter was crossing barriers in her military career. And he had finally begun to confront the possibility that she enjoyed her role in what was traditionally a man's world. Carol's reports from advanced training had even made him replay in his mind the few stories Mid had told him about carrying donuts to the troops back in the war. Mid then and Carol now made close female friends. Had his wife enjoyed her women comrades more then than she liked being with him now?

He thought about Curtis and his relationships with women. He had not come home at all this fall, so his dates with Sarah Bridges must have, as Oscar had hoped, turned into a "summer romance." Curtis wrote mostly about his classes and the part-time job he'd found at a garden shop. He was planting seeds in peat pots, transferring plants into pots, tagging plants for sale.

"It's boring work, but I only have to do it in two-hour stretches," he explained. "Then I get to man the desk while the owners are shutting everything down for the night. I'm grateful I don't have to work out on their farm. *That's* hard labor! But there are bands of hippies in their psychedelic vans crisscrossing the country to pick and pack our fruit."

Oscar worried that his younger son might hitch a ride with these dropouts and end up in some commune out in California. He knew the professors at Westminster were liberals who challenged basic tenets of the American system, making free love and protest admirable activities. He felt they were undermining the very system that paid their salaries.

Thank goodness he taught at South Central State, thought Oscar, where the rigor of math and science courses weeds out those not serious about their education. Jan Reynolds, now. That was the kind of girl Curtis should team up with--sensible, organized, focused. With her chemistry degree, she could teach and still be home after the school day to take care of children.

But Oscar couldn't worry about all that right now. He had to figure out how to find a replacement set designer. He wandered out to the kitchen. Then he went back to the family room and clicked on the Zenith. Finally, he broke down and called Mid. "Could you come down for a bit? I could use some advice."

# Chapter Thirty-two: Figures

If the house on Middlecourt Road had seemed large when he and Mid inspected it last spring, now it felt enormous. Four full-size bedrooms (they'd had two on Limestone Drive, with his small office in the basement and part of the attic made into children rooms), a living room and family room (only a living room in the other house), two-car rather than single garage, and a kitchen as large as the old one plus the adjacent small dining room. And all on one floor.

As they had positioned their furniture in the summer, each piece was liberated from cluttered surroundings; and the family had room to walk without bumping into coffee table, lamp, or footstool. There were walls to spread their pictures out, closets larger than their wardrobes (with spare ones in the extra bedrooms), spacious cabinets built into family room, kitchen, and utility room.

And, of course, once the kids went back to school and Carol was off with the Army, it had been just the two of them. Now Oscar would wander the length of the house, peer into open spaces, hear his footsteps echo down the hall, choose from half a dozen places to sit or recline. He felt like the last man on earth.

Waiting for Mid to come down from Ellie's, he was surprised to hear the phone (it seemed to be ringing less and less). It was Louis asking for his mother.

"She's at a neighbor's right now," Oscar explained. "Can she call you back in an hour?"

"Sure." Louis hesitated. "I . . . uh, I guess could ask your opinion."

"I suspect this is not a matter of physics or math. Still, I'll give it my best shot."

Oscar knew all his children shared their personal concerns more with Mid than with him. He did not mean to discourage such confidences but had come to recognize that something about him--aloof demeanor, rigid posture, formal manner of speaking?-- discouraged many people, even his own children, from opening up to him. Students or colleagues rarely came to him about romantic crises, family issues, so-called "peer pressure." And, a member of no social organizations or civic groups, his circle of acquaintances was small. Another of his reasons for directing a play might be to change others' perceptions of him.

Louis went on. "Well, not that I'm ready to do this, you understand, but a bunch of us were talking the other day about wedding proposals. You've never talked much about how you popped the question to Mom, and I was just wondering how most men go about it--in real life, of course, not as we see it in the movies."

"Ah, on the silver screen it's on bended knee at a candlelit dinner by the ocean. He pulls a diamond ring

238

from his jacket pocket, and she gasps with pleasure." Oscar knew this was a cliché, overused in B-grade movies. His own favorite versions never followed that pattern.

"Yes," agreed Louis. "But law students can't afford expensive rings, or even dinners at fashionable restaurants."

Oscar recalled the quirky off-stage offer of marriage a moody Laurence Olivier makes to an unhappy Joan Fontaine in *Rebecca*. He's actually off-screen in a bathroom, his voice carrying at first a coded proposal, then a direct one. She's taken off guard.

"To tell the truth, I believe most declarations of love are not planned, or, if planned, stray from the script. Everyone's too nervous to behave exactly as they think they will. And if they weren't, I'd say their feelings were not genuine."

"So, did you surprise Mom, lead up to the moment with subtle hints, or just blurt it out without even intending to?"

"Well, it was a long time ago," Oscar said. "We hadn't known each other very long, and my memory is that we sort of knew we would get married without ever saying it out loud."

"Interesting. Did the times--it was wartime, wasn't it?--did that sort of wipe out the usual rules for courtship?"

Oscar mused. Back then he had tended to dismiss the news of what was going on in Europe and Asia as irrelevant to his own life; and he ignored signs that his country was likely to be drawn into conflict. Both his parents had been isolationists, concentrating on surviving the Depression themselves and then seeing their son rise in American society.

"It *was* a special time. A lot of men thought they might die overseas and so wanted to enjoy romance before it was too late--either ahead of or in marriage. So, yes, there were short engagements, even elopements."

"Well," laughed Louis, "Carol is taking care of any family military obligation and doesn't seem much interested in proposing to anyone. But back to you and Mom—"

"I guess the short answer to your question is that I left a proposal on the back of a postcard on her desk at the health department. Pretty straightforward; it said, 'Marry me.'"

Louis chuckled again. "Right to the point, what I'd expect from the scientist. Still, I think there must have been some lead-up. I'll see what Mom says. Get her to call if she has a minute."

After he'd hung up, Oscar wandered the house again. He hadn't wanted to tell his son that, when he and Mid first met, she had been more experienced at romance than he--or at least at serious romance. He'd had a number of flirtations in college, but nothing that went on for any length of time. Whenever he thought back to that period of his youth, he was dismayed to see himself as indecisive, reserved, almost timid, though there were reasons.

In the master bedroom he studied himself in the mirror over his dresser. Only in his mid-forties, he looked fit, bright-eyed, engaged. And professionally at least, he possessed a confidence based on a fine teaching record, numerous publications in perhaps the most challenging field of science, and a reviving sense of his artistic ability.

On the corner of the dresser sat a small cylindrical glass case. He could see the back reflected in the lower left hand corner of the mirror. A brown ball on the top allowed him to lift the glass and view directly two tiny figurines--a bride in her wedding dress holding her bouquet and a groom in his tuxedo, hair parted down the middle in the style of the 1940s.

He and Mid had eloped, taking the train from Jefferson City to Kansas City, finding a justice of the peace, and calling the rest of that weekend their honeymoon. They telephoned their respective parents just before boarding the return train late at night. Their actions were excused because, as Louis had surmised, many people were taking impulsive actions in anticipation of an uncertain future. But Mid and Oscar were acting without regard to current events.

Mid was not an ostentatious person. And the last of three sisters to marry, she didn't feel the need for an elaborate affair. Oscar enjoyed getting the attention of others, but he was conscious some might recognize that he was considerably younger than his bride. All he wanted was to take Mid home with him and begin the rest of their lives together. (Actually, they would live at her place, which was roomier and better furnished.) There were no pictures from the wedding, only the little figurines the colleagues at the health department surprised them with after they returned.

How did they reach the point where he could leave the "Marry me" message on her desk and they could sneak away from everyone they knew to marry?

Oscar admitted to himself that his courtship of Marian Lacy might have been characterized as inept. She was the one who perceived his desire, returned his love, and waited expectantly for a proposal that he lacked the courage to make. She would not realize for some time why he was so unsure of himself at that stage of his life.

His college career had been interrupted when his father, a carpenter and builder, was injured and unable to work for the better part of two years. Oscar was hired at Wesleyan as a research associate, and his income helped his parents get through the last years of the Depression. But having been told all his life that he was destined for great things, he suffered a loss of confidence.

He had been the best student in most of his courses, no matter what the field. And, if he hadn't broken his wrist in a fight with Tank Thompson, he might also have become a classical pianist. For two years he was on the staff of the college, not one of its star pupils. At times he felt barely above the level of custodians and groundskeepers.

When he graduated, he was offered a fellowship to a graduate program in mathematics at the University of Washington. But that was so far away, he feared his mother would suffer another nervous breakdown and his father the burden of caring for her. So, he traveled to Jefferson City, where his mother had family, for a job in the state health department.

Wooing the more experienced and beautiful woman newly arrived from the East was intimidating, and he could only do so by indirection and humor. Rather than the bold stroke he characterized it, his "Marry me" note really was more an act of desperation by a man who could not speak out directly.

And now he felt he was need of another desperate gesture.

# Chapter Thirty-three:
# Lenses

"Hello, Oscar," Mid said coming into the bedroom. "What is it that you need? Can't get your eye out again?"

Oscar had no trouble inserting his contact lens, but he often had great difficulty getting it out. "No, not tonight. And I've asked you not to call it my 'eye.'"

"Okay, okay. What is it that I can do for you?"

"Well, I guess, first, you'd better call Louis. He wanted to talk to you about how we got engaged. I gave him my version, but you will probably want to set the record straight."

"I suspect I know what this is about. He's going to propose to Suzanne." Still in the doorway, she was leafing through the stack of mail he'd left for her by front door. "Okay, I'll call from the kitchen phone. Then we'll talk about your problems."

Why did she have to say "problems"? She made it sound as if he couldn't get through a day without being rescued several times. He was doing quite all right with the important things. But no one would be prepared to take on the series of misfortunes directing a play had inspired.

Oscar stepped into the master bathroom. He hadn't, in fact, gotten his contact lens out, and he decided he'd better take care of that now—just in case.

The lens had been prescribed after the cataract surgery, a standard procedure at the time; and Oscar had been hopeful it would significantly improve his vision, which had been weak since childhood. But the darn thing fit so tightly on his eyeball that Dr. Letts finally provided him with a special device--sort of a miniature plunger--to help. A small stick with a tiny suction cup at the end, it worked fine so long as his hand was still. And there was less chance of losing it when he transferred the lens to the small plastic storage case than when stuck on a fingertip.

Contact lens surgery at this time was not routine, and complications could occur during or after the operation. Because of the glass' impermeability, no oxygen is transmitted to the conjunctiva and cornea, and irritation was one of the milder possible reactions. Oscar felt he'd been fortunate overall.

Taking several deep breaths to steady himself, he rinsed the plunger in a cleaning solution, aimed it at his eyeball, and wondered why he was afflicted with this irritation. He might be on the cusp of a new wave of personal accomplishment, almost a second career, at the same time he sustained an older record of achievement. Conventional wisdom held that mathematicians did their most significant work when young, in their twenties; but writers--or so many believed--continued to improve with age.

Opening his eye as wide as he could, Oscar tilted his head this way and that so the light reflected off the edge of the lens and he could determine exactly where it sat on the cornea. Hitting dead center was the goal.

Oscar imagined himself writing scripts for television, giving talks to community theater groups, teaching drama seminars to eager would-be playwrights. Bright young faces would look up to take in the words of this rare combination of the scientist and the humanist, a man who could connect the mysteries of the physical universe with the longings of the human heart.

"There!" he whispered, gently tilting the plunger and lifting the lens off the surface of his eyeball. He blinked away a few tears, and prized the lens into the case. "Done."

He imagined himself as Dylan Thomas, the Welsh poet whose striking verse evoked unrestrained emotion. Though Thomas' personal life was tortured by marital infidelities, financial struggles, and alcoholic binges, he had been praised by erudite scholars and idolized by young women. He wrote for radio and movies but was more famous for his public performances. His intoxicated readings in America after the war intoxicated listeners.

Would Oscar's own story--following a carpenter father and farm girl mother across the plains looking for work during the Depression--be material for another profound exploration of passion and desire? How about the struggles of a brilliant young student forced to drop out of college and earn money when his father is injured back in the home country?

Oscar asked himself, how is it that "Fern Hill" ends? *"Oh as I was young and easy in the mercy of his means / Time held me green and dying / Though I sang in my chains like the sea"*? He thought about the chains of his own childhood--boring schools, storerooms where he worked odd jobs, family dinner tables with decent but ordinary people. And he remembered the longings for achievement, distinction, some kind of stardom.

How he would like now to explore the sensitive soul of a young man with the wind off the prairie stirring dreams of immortality! He could show how the methods of science restricted a man's heart (which would be breaking free decades later) and exposed a flaw in the American way of life. He would show his countrymen that they were abusing unprecedented prosperity by becoming a society of unrestrained materialists.

"I was right," said Mid. She had come into the bedroom and sat down on the edge of their bed. Oscar started, not having heard her approach. "But I don't think he'll propose just yet or that they'll marry for another year."

He returned to his dresser, as if he needed to make sure he had clean clothes for tomorrow. "Oh—yes, Louis. Well, I think she'll take good care of him."

"Another postcard from Carol," Mid mused. "She doesn't seem to have time to write anything longer. How does she sound to you?"

"The same, I guess. Busy, busy, busy."

"Did you know she asked about Aaron in her last phone call? And here she tells us to thank the boys for their cards."

"What do you mean? You think she misses friends and family or regrets her decision?"

"Maybe. Hard to say." She stepped over to set the mail on her dresser. "So?"

"Oh, me. Yeah, well, maybe I just need someone to sympathize, but, Jackson, buildings and grounds, quit as set designer today. There's not much time for someone to come up with a new plan and execute it."

"Why did he quit?"

"His wife has to have surgery on her back and will be bedridden for a month. He says he can't afford someone to take care of her, but in my opinion, that may just be an excuse. Still, he was the only experienced person interested in taking on *Little Sheba*. The other veterans were already committed to later productions."

"So, it's design, construction, operation?"

"Right. A major ingredient for success!"

"Hmm. I do know someone. You might not be interested, but—"

"I'm desperate. There are enough other problems--temperamental actors, schedule conflicts--that this might sink everything. And I'm certainly no set builder."

248

Oscar, in fact, never knew if he had inherited any of his father's talent for figuring out the structure needed in a particular situation, the materials necessary to build it, the method of construction. His mother had insisted he stay out of his father's shop, as he was destined for a higher calling. And Carl, knowing how hard he had worked to establish himself in the trade--and to survive hard times--agreed. Oscar should move into the professional classes.

Mid asked, "Could the position be shared? I mean, if two people worked together, that wouldn't be a problem for you, would it?"

Around the house it had always been Mid who supervised professional workman on major jobs (putting two small bedrooms and a half bath in the attic of their former house) and took on minor construction tasks herself (fencing in an area for the family dog, installing a ladder on the garage wall by which one could reach storage areas above, assembling and painting unfinished dressers for the children).

"Two people, three, a committee, so long as there's a key person I can work with."

"Okay. You've got yourself a volunteer. And Ellie will be a partner."

"Ellie — and — ?

"Ellie and me. Maybe I've never told you, but I worked on several productions in college. I had a good friend who was a theater major, and I liked teaming with her."

Oscar didn't quite know what to say. "So now you'd be working with Ellie—and with me. Would you like that? We're not working together here," he waved his hand at the room, "very well."

"Oscar, I have moved in with Ellie for a time, yes. But you and I haven't decided on our future. We've not told anyone about this, not even our children. Ellie needs my company, especially at night; and—you know how I felt you didn't need mine. But, if I can help you through this play, that's just—something we can do for right now."

# Chapter Thirty-four: Herds

"Let me tell you a little story," Harold Miller said to Oscar one day in the next week. The younger man knew the older one was not literally asking permission to launch into a narrative. "It may help you think differently about becoming chairman."

When Harold stopped by his office, Oscar worried that some complaint about how he was handling *Come Back, Little Sheba* had made its way to the department head. With fast-changing policies about members of one family working at the same state institution, he wondered if there could be objections to Mid's becoming set designer, even though no money was involved.

Once he realized the topic was who would succeed Harold, Oscar replied with relief, "Sure. I'm always ready to listen." He leaned back in his chair, convinced that he could deflect Harold with a surprise suggestion. (That didn't mean, though, that he would necessarily turn down a similar position at Enchantment College should he receive an offer.)

Oscar had always liked and admired Harold as an able administrator. But two little things occasionally irritated him. The first was his way of trying to make a simple point with a complex story. They were both scientists, for heaven's sake! Just say what you mean directly.

"You know," Harold began, "I came here from industry, having worked in labs and then directing one for about ten years."

"Right. Your connections have certainly benefitted us. With you as liaison, we've gotten contracts for research with Fairfield industries and down at Fort Wood." Funding from federal and corporate sources outside state government was increasingly important to his colleagues and to the university. "I, of course, have none of that experience."

"Yes. Well, when I was brought in, it was thought my background would immediately open up job opportunities for our graduates and research possibilities for faculty. It didn't happen, though, for several years. I'm afraid I didn't understand how academics operate, which is much different than scientists employed in the business sector."

"I would have to admit faculty don't see themselves as workers taking orders from bosses. But we do all belong to the same organization and work toward common goals."

The other of Harold's irritating traits was inexplicable: he pronounced a single word oddly. "Buffalo" always came out "Bluffalo." It made Oscar think Miller's version of that city in New York rested on a high cliffs above Lake Erie or the Niagara River. Even famous Niagara Falls, though, twenty miles to the north, fell only 167 feet from top to bottom.

"It took me a few years," Harold went on, "but I did begin to figure out some strategies. It was actually my boyhood experience in agriculture that gave me a clue."

"I think I know the lesson from farming mushrooms: 'feed them manure and keep them in the dark.'"

Harold seemed puzzled. "No, never heard that. I used what I learned about sheep and cattle."

Oscar and his friend Bill Rust had a standing wager on when, in a department meeting or casual conversation, the word "Buffalo"/"Bluffalo" would come up. It seemed incredible that the topic appeared with some frequency. Of course, each man tried to make it happen.

"You know, that reminds me," Oscar observed. "I read recently that some Western ranchers are considering raising bison for meat as a beef substitute."

"Now, I have heard about that. All that open space, of course, is their natural habitat. And since they became protected, their numbers have grown."

"But you wanted to talk about the department chairmanship. Now, I don't want you think I'll try to confuse, bewilder, or hoodwink anyone, but Bill Rust might just be our man."

Harold raised an eyebrow, not, hoped Oscar, because of his wording but because of his surprising suggestion. "Interesting. But let me go back to the farm a minute."

Even as he listened, Oscar began to think how many times he had been maneuvered--even stampeded (as a buffalo)--into places he never wanted to be. He rethought his proposal to Mid. Was it possible he had let himself be herded into matrimony?

Oscar had arrived in Jefferson City fresh out of college and eager for romance. He knew none of the girls he would meet there would know him as the son of a carpenter, someone who had had to drop out of school to support his family. Instead, they would see a young man who could play the saxophone, work math problems faster than anyone, throw combination punches to the gut and jaw. It was inevitable that he would win the most beautiful girl he met.

"So," said Harold, "every day I had to get those forty sheep from the far pasture back close to the barn, where our dogs could protect them through the night. Stern, our collie, and I would wear ourselves out circling that herd, trying to get them up the path. I was convinced if I could get Superior--he was the biggest ram out there--moving out in front, the rest would follow. Shows what I knew about animal behavior!"

"Superior now--he was unusually large? Almost like a cow or something of that size?"

Oscar knew now that, as a boy, he had built up a fantasy about the girl he would marry. From movie stars and heroines in romantic novels, he created an image that Mid uncannily matched--the eyes, the hair, the smile. When he first saw her at the health department, he didn't realize she had already become

254

a part of his dream. The attractive East Coast native had crossed his path in a little St. Louis bookstore a decade earlier. So striking was that encounter to Oscar that he'd written a song about the memory of that young beauty--"Route 66 Sweetheart."

He later submitted the song in a contest. He became so wrapped up in the romance of his composition that, finding her address in Rutherford, New Jersey, he wrote the woman, Marian Lacy, asking for a picture. Winning this prize, he explained, would help him continue his education. He received the photo in the mail more quickly than he had dared hope.

"But here's a fact for you, Oscar," said Harold. "The leader of a herd isn't the one out front. The others somehow recognize his importance and keep him in the middle of the group, protecting him. And the leader does his directing from that position."

"Ah."

"I had to learn that about faculty, too--not to seem belittling, as they're not sheep. But the most outspoken--I don't mean Arthur James now, you know I don't--the most outspoken is often being led by someone who doesn't stand out--the way, I think, you often position yourself."

"So," Oscar said to Harold, "it seems to me you're thinking of William, too. He keeps a low profile in meetings, but understands very well what's going on. You probably don't know as well as I do how in one-on-one meetings he shapes opinions in the department."

Harold rubbed his chin, a habitual gesture when he felt people were deliberately not understanding him. Oscar had seen him do it many times with Charlotte. Mid explained that Harold's wife was probably the only one who'd learned how to handle him. When Oscar called Mid "Sarge," he meant it to be ironical; but he knew she had her ways of getting what she wanted from him, too.

When he met Marian (nicknamed "Mid") that second time in Jefferson City, Oscar felt his dream had appeared in the flesh. He was in a rush to become the love of her life. In all his fantasized encounters of such a moment, he was captivating, she swept away by his charms. But now, when the time actually came, he stuttered and stumbled while she was amused and knowing. His sly hints caused only a raised eyebrow, not a blushing duck of her head. The subtle fishing for compliments produced an easy change of subject.

"'The Undertones had a raunchy crowd last night," he would say to her, referring to the jazz combo he played in with his cousins. "Had to quiet them with an incredibly sweet rendition of 'Let Me Call You Sweetheart'—sweetheart." He added the second "sweetheart" as if he were idly repeating the last word of the title—but perhaps, just perhaps, calling her sweetheart.

"How does that go?" she asked innocently. And suddenly he couldn't remember the lyrics.

"Anyway, Oscar," concluded Harold, "You have all the ability to be a good department chairman. You've been leading without many of your colleagues realizing it. But as chairman, you'd get credit for doing it. And a nice boost in salary I'm sure Mid will appreciate."

"Marry me," Oscar had written years earlier on the back of the picture Mid had sent him. He had little real hope at the time that she would. Now he asked if he had brought himself to that point or had she drawn him?

"Well, time for me to shuffle off," said Harold and rose to leave. "You be thinking."

When he was out the door and in the hall, Oscar asked himself, "Did he just say 'shluffle'"?

# Thirty-five: Waters

"So, what they call a 'waterfront' lot is a third of an acre bordering a creek?" Oscar was gazing downhill through a thin stand of scrub oak to a rocky creek bed. He could see stakes for similar lots on both sides of the one he was viewing. Across the way, the ground was flat for about twenty feet and then rose steeply. There were no markers on that side.

Mid explained. "The water will be coming up on the other side because of some new landscaping they've done." She pointed. "It could be about twenty-five feet across in that low spot. Certainly enough water to float a canoe down to the lake itself."

"Ah, all part of the magnificent Avalon Lake Homes. You know Avalon is a mythical place. They say King Arthur was carried there after his last, fatal battle with Mordred, to a land that's shrouded in mist. I think this development's future is cloudy, too."

"I thought you liked that sort of romantic setting. Can't you picture yourself, knight in shining armor, boarding some ancient barque and heading off on an adventure?"

"I think I'd rather read about it. Okay, now that I've seen it, what do we do next?"

Oscar wasn't sure why he'd agreed to come in the first place. Maybe it was his effort to pay her back for taking on the set design (which, it quickly became clear, she and Ellie knew how to do). Mid had learned about this spot from a real estate agent whose clock she had restored and proposed she and Oscar take a Sunday drive that way, observing the fall colors on the way.

When they had first come to Fairfield--and gas was less than thirty cents a gallon--they used to take such weekend drives, often with the children. It was official small town recreation. Maybe Mid was suggesting a return to happier days.

He knew the idea of a summer place on the water also reminded her of her childhood, camping from mid-June to September on Greenwood Lake in upstate New Jersey. The family had finally sold their land this year for a very good price. None of the grandchildren was interested in building, and development there had accelerated.

Mid explained, "A vacation home could be part of my future or our future. That's what we're considering, Oscar. Ellie is thinking of buying and building and would like a partner."

"You would do this without me?"

"I don't really know. We've reached some sort of crisis, you and I, in the way forward--or maybe it's the way backward. You're resurrecting your college music and playwriting career, and I'm returning to the role of housewife without children."

He looked back at his car, worried that rough roads might have thrown up rocks and chipped the paint. Her moving out had been, he felt, drastic, "utility-ization" carried to an extreme. He said, "You know, Arthur was supposed to return, healed from his wounds, take up his sword and the crown. I'd like to think I'm just picking up some past interests that were put aside for a time. They can carry me--or us--forward."

Mid turned to look where the creek wound through trees down toward the lake. "I want to be more than a sidekick on your journey. I need to have my own interests, like clock repair, or to share more fully in yours. Buying this lot, designing a small retirement house, that's something we could do together. The two of us did build one life as a couple—"

Oscar had quietly celebrated when the fall semester began and he could claim he was too busy to help arranging the new house. He wanted to come home every day to stability and order, even more once the play began to take up his spare time and the politicking about the department chair increased. Establishing a home away from home would rob him of weekends and summers.

Mid mused, "You know, there are stories about Camelot coming again. Ellie tells me C. S. Lewis wrote that the king was alive and well, just on Venus. You like science fiction. That idea might appeal to you."

Oscar thought about Roger's and his own interest in the made-up worlds of Edgar Rice Burroughs. For him those fantasies were simply escape and carried no moral lessons. "Lewis could spin a tale, but the Christian preaching always leaves me cold."

She sighed. "These may be times when we need a few sermons.

"Oscar scowled. "You can guess that I'm not likely to look for guidance from organized religion, no matter how — difficult our situation might be."

Oscar wondered if Ellie, faithful member of Fairfield's Lutheran church, was influencing Mid. Before they separated, she and her husband offered to take the Lindblooms anytime they wanted to see what that service was like, but Oscar made it clear he was not interested.

"You may need some guidance from somewhere," Mid said, turning toward him and planting her feet apart. "Oscar, there's something I need to tell you."

"You've already bought this land? With Ellie?" Actually, he didn't see how she could have, as they had only the one joint checking account. However, he remembered, she was expecting a share of the profits from the sale of the Greenwood Lake property.

"No, it's not about Avalon Lake Homes. It's about Carol."

"Carol?" This was an unexpected change of topic."Yes, Carol. She was pregnant."

He was frozen. "Pregnant? Was?"

"Yes, up until a few weeks ago. She — lost the baby." Mid turned away to look at the hillside.

He reached out for her arm. "But she's all right, isn't she? I mean, health and all?"

"Yes." She turned back to him. "She's recovered completely. It was—sudden and quick."

Oscar thought. "You can't have a baby and be a soldier, can you? What happened? And who was the father. When I find out—" He clinched a fist.

"You're not going to find out. Neither am I. Carol is a legal adult, and what she does is her own business."

Oscar's head was spinning. His daughter pregnant? Some boy slept with her? She'd been carrying the baby while she was in the Army? It made no sense.

"I'll be damned if it's not my business!" exploded Oscar. "I'm going out there tomorrow—or at the end of the week. Someone took advantage of my daughter. I mean, I guess —was she—attacked?"

"Rape" was a word Oscar could not say easily in front of a woman, even Mid. Physical violence of men against men--fist fights, combat--occurred in the world he understood. But that such a thing would happen to his child was unimaginable. His daughter, a girl with more brains than anyone in her high school class! Maybe than anyone in Fairfield.

"Oscar, it was nothing like that. She thought she—she thought they—had taken the appropriate precautions."

Oscar stared. "She—they. Je-sus *Christ*!"

"The world is changing, Oscar, whether we like it or not. This is not going to jeopardize her military career. No one in her outfit knows. And we're not going to mention it to anyone."

He turned it over in his mind. "So — so, you could have decided not to tell me, leave me in the dark. I could have thought of her the way she was — before, as the child who was going to be the mathematician in the family, someone who would continue the — tradition."

"Carol and I thought it wouldn't be honest. Both her parents should know, however painful it would be."

Oscar realized he'd been out of the loop for weeks, maybe even before Mid had starting staying nights at Ellie's. For all he knew, Mid had traveled to see Carol after she lost the baby.

He tried to assemble what he understood about miscarriages, especially ones coming early in pregnancy. There would have been signs, bleeding or whatnot, months before her water would break. But things must have been far enough along for her to know something was wrong, that what she was experiencing was not some other "feminine complaint."

My God, that very term revealed how little he knew of such matters! He'd worried about what his sons might do after puberty. And he understood that physiology quite well. But what occurred in women's bodies was largely a mystery.

"Can we go home now?" he asked Mid. "I don't think I'm ready to make an offer on—" he gestured, "on this."

"Of course. And I apologize somewhat for using this trip to break the news to you. I thought getting out of the familiar, regular world would—I don't know, be appropriate."

Oscar sighed. "Well, at least there's not enough water here for me to wade in with all my armor on!"

# Chapter Thirty-Six: Drives

"So," concluded Oscar that night, sitting in his study and staring at the sheet of music he'd composed for Rockers of Age. "So, here I am, living alone in a four-bedroom, two-garage house on half an acre of land. One of my children is planning to marry a Catholic girl and in the future will probably visit here only for a day or so. My young daughter, having known a lover, is in the military and may serve many years overseas. And my middle child has no real idea what he wants to do with his life, but he'll figure it out without my guidance. It must be time for a drink."

He failed to acknowledge that, although his wife had not slept here in a month, tonight she was here. As they approached Fairfield on the new interstate, Mid had said, "It's been a shock, I know, Carol's . . difficulties. You might want to talk—later in the evening."

He felt it was just a gesture, more a pause in the withdrawal he was beginning to feel was inevitable. She and Ellie would buy vacation property and set up housekeeping together. Two divorced women, tired of their husbands, were taking charge of their lives.

Not wanting to admit that he couldn't cope on his own, he told Mid he would be fine at home alone. Gesturing at the road ahead, he said, "They claim that because this new highway follows the same path as Route 66, it's not going to change the shape of town. But since you can't get to 'roadside attractions' without taking an exit and doubling back, I think the older, established businesses along the highway are going to be in trouble."

"You mean like the Teepee Toy Store and Shady Grove Motel? I'm not sure Fairfield needs them anyway." They'd never been in the Shady Grove, the Teepee only once. But on many a leisurely drive years ago, they'd chuckled as they drove past.

Teepee sold conventional souvenirs--hillbilly corncob pipes, Route 66 keychains, mass-produced Ozark crafts--but also had a back room with erotic magazine, toys for the bedroom, and a local moonshine labeled "Show-Me Elixir." The Shady Grove was shady in not asking couples of any age for identification. Still, they were both familiar institutions.

"You have a point about some of our less reputable establishments, but the new chain motels and restaurants are already putting up giant billboards." He pointed to a row of three ahead of them. "Small, locally-owned places like Stony Court can't afford to compete with that kind of advertising. The future is coming, and I'm not sure I like it."

"The town will have to hold on to what makes it distinctive, I guess. The university continues to draw good students and build ties with industry, so you're a good part of the area's future. Ellie told me Harold wants you to be the next department chair. Is that going to happen?"

"I certainly hope not. I've recommended Bill."

She huffed. "He'll never take it. He's created the ultimate nuclear family, living out in the country and teaching his daughters at home. The job takes more social skills than he has."

"That's another reason I'm not interested in taking it on. I've never been a 'hail fellow, well met' guy. I'm going to tell Bill it could be an avenue to promotion for him; and certainly the salary will help him send his girls to college. They're not going to earn any scholarships!"

Oscar traced the Rust sisters' lackluster academic performance to their mother, a sweet woman Bill had grown up with. She'd gone to work as a secretary at eighteen and, like a lot of girls at the time, never aspired to a greater career. For Oscar, IQ scores were the basic measure of ability; and Bill's genes had lost the battle with Sally's.

All three Lindbloom children had tested in the 90% range. Carol, with the highest score, could claim to be a genius. Although he admired Mid's abilities, believing her by far the smartest of the three Lacy sisters, Oscar assumed his genes determined the family's future.

"You want to stop and get something to eat?" asked Mid as they took the new exit into town. "Or I could come back with you and fix something?"

"I suppose we could stop at Smokey Joe's. I wouldn't want you to have to cook, and I could use a break from warmed up leftovers." Since she moved in with Ellie, Mid had been preparing casseroles and freezing meal-size portions for Oscar. He also had a supply of TV dinners. Even in his present circumstances, Oscar wasn't going to learn to cook.

Joe's, once a drive-in A & W root beer stand, perched on the hill north of Fairfield on old Route 66. The new, four-lane highway was straighter and descended the Gasconade plateau more gradually than had its predecessor. It seemed to Oscar that the land had been sliced in two by some giant machine, two concrete strips of highway bracketed by more strips of access road.

When they were settled in a booth, Mid asked him, "What did you do about the Enchantment College position? Are you going to apply?"

"It might be an attractive opportunity. If—if things here are becoming—are no longer satisfactory here, it might be best for me to move on."

She studied the menu. "We've done okay with the play. You approved the design Ellie and I drew up, and it's nice that you're just letting us go ahead on our own."

"I've got my hands full with the actors. Melissa, now—she's been in so many local productions I didn't think she'd be a problem at all."

"I've noticed how often she wants your opinion. Of course, you are the director."

"She wants too much coaching for a theater veteran, asking about every scene. I mean, I do have my ideas about how Lola should be portrayed. She's loyal and long-suffering, but Melissa keeps trying to show her as—I don't know, frustrated."

"Frustrated with herself or her husband?"

"Frustrated as in wanting more romance in her life. But she and Doc have been married too long for that. They're a partnership, not red-hot lovers."

"So," Mid mused. "So, maybe she's incorporating today's new ideas about women into Lola's role, suggesting that, even though she's middle-aged, she has her own—desires."

Oscar realized that Melissa often wanted to talk to him privately, that she was often taking him by the arm, asking questions about her character, hoping he was pleased with her performance. When he answered, she'd squeeze his arm and tell him how wise he was.

"Well, this looks good," he said, spreading his napkin across his lap. "So, are you still writing the kids every week?" This was a tradition Mid had inherited from her mother.

"Yes. At times I feel a bit of a hypocrite, though. We're going to have to make some decisions pretty soon, I think, and maybe bring them into the conversation. So far, everyone here thinks I'm just being kind to Ellie by spending nights there. But the talk is bound to change."

"You know I don't want you to stay away. I was hoping a break would help you see that we're better together." He spooned some gravy over his mashed potatoes. "I never quite understood what happened anyway. I've done as I've always done--worked, come home. The house is pretty empty, though, now. The kids' rooms, the clock repair factory — "

Mid looked past him toward the front entrance, the parking area and the street beyond. "As I've said, we need to be more than joint occupants of the same house. Even when you're there, I often feel like I'm alone. When they talk about 'empty nest' syndrome, I think it's something parents feel about the absent children, not each other."

Oscar didn't know how to answer. It was all he could do to keep up with teaching and research. Other men, like Harold, could sustain outside interests, like a farm. But Oscar needed the comfort and security of home to recover from each day--not because he was aging, but because he had done it so long.

"Mid, maybe I don't say it enough, but I miss them all enormously. It's been a shock, coming home to an empty house every day. And now, you're not there — and Carol. Oh, my!"

Mid put a hand on his hand. "Are you sure you don't want me to stay tonight? I can work on the grandfather clock mechanism I bought at the auction. Ellie won't be back until the middle of the day tomorrow, anyway." She'd gone to visit her son and his family in St. Louis.

"Well, I guess I would like that."

270

She looked hard at him. "One more thing: if you're thinking Aaron had—had anything to do with this, you're wrong. In fact, his fiancée arrived in town this fall. He and Carol were good friends, but never a couple."

Later, as Oscar stared at the sheet music in front of him, he thought of Mid only a few rooms away, mounting gears, adjusting arbors, getting works in beat. She would sleep over, but he knew it would be in Carol's bed. Still, she was in the house.

He called the song he wrote "A Lover's Lament" to reflect Doc's state of mind late in the play. The morning after an alcoholic binge, in which he nearly kills his wife, Doc fears Lola will leave him. Oscar's song is a melancholy, self-centered tune of regret. Doc and Oscar loose themselves in a dreamy improvisation.

# Chapter Thirty-seven: Grabs

Oscar's proposal to Bill Rust was not well received. "What are you trying to do to me?" his friend asked. "You know I don't want to be department chair. Plus I'd do a terrible job."

"Well, my first argument is that Arthur James wants it."

"That's a strong reason for anyone else to be chair, but not for me to be in that position. Why isn't your hat in the ring? After all, you've been here your whole career; you know the faculty and the administration; you understand how things get done. Harold wants you, too, which would get you in good with deans and vice presidents."

Oscar swiveled his desk chair ninety degrees so he could look out the window. He hadn't wanted the job when Harold first surprised him with the idea. Since then his personal problems had mounted--his daughter "in trouble," his wife disaffected at best, his sons increasingly distant. But he couldn't tell even as close a friend as Bill about such private family matters.

"Look. I don't want to be crude about this, but the position comes with a substantial increase in salary. Your girls will be needing your help financially for at least four more years. And a lot of faculty have used administrative experience to get promotions. You can look at this as quite an opportunity."

Bill frowned. "Oscar, it may be hard for you to believe--having just bought yourself a new house and saddled yourself with a big mortgage--but my home is already paid for. As you know, I only built it as I had the cash available. We lived in the basement for seven years. And the twins are ready to work their way through college."

Oscar hadn't been ready for this information, especially as it touched a sore point--how he'd locked himself in with this new house. Though he and Mid had always been frugal, it would still take ten years to pay off the mortgage.

"Well, that's—that's good, even admirable. Still, you don't know what's coming down the road." He leaned closer to Bill and winked. "I had one of those strange brown envelopes in my faculty box this week, and who knows when I'll have to hire a high-priced lawyer to keep me out of jail for possession of obscene material."

As incongruous as it would seem to anyone who knew Bill superficially, he owned a substantial collection of pornographic magazines. Whether he subscribed under an alias or picked them up in some disreputable shop--probably near Fort Leonard Wood--Oscar didn't know. But every now and then he would leave one labeled "Confidential" in Oscar's box.

"Ah, Miss November perhaps?"

"That would be her." Oscar pointed to the leather briefcase in the chair of his typing table. He could lock the case, and he always took Bill's gifts home immediately. He had a hiding place in an old cabinet his father had made, but he didn't like to keep them there long. He worried not about skeletons in his closets but pictures of naked women behind a sliding panel.

"Wait until you see what I have for you next. There's a new magazine called *BassAckwards* that's not as discreet as *Playboy*."

Oscar didn't like to admit that he was always curious about what would be in these magazines. The better known ones had become predictable--beautiful, naked or near naked women in provocative poses. Others, harder to find, went further. He predicted men would soon appear in the pictures grabbing the parts of women.

"You laugh, but my collection is going to be worth a fortune one day. Standards are changing, and there'll come a time when such things are readily available to anyone. Men, women, even adolescents with cash provided by their indulgent parents will be able to purchase them on the open market."

"I hope I don't live to see that day!"

While Oscar was curious about the magazines, since adolescence he had generally filled out his erotic fantasies with classic written works. Those could sit in the bookshelves of his den appropriately filed in alphabetical order according to title. The graphic color images of *Playboy* left his imagination less room to shape his ideals.

Bill explained, "I find the trends fascinating. From racy novels like *Lady Chatterley's Lover*, written by a literary giant, the twentieth century has opened up to trashy pictures in magazines written at a sixth-grade level. The secrets of erotica are hidden no more."

Oscar suspected he was right. While he'd didn't go off in the war to see Paris like many in his generation, he know that some came home with decks of pornographic playing cards and obscene comic books. Now the market offered more racy material. Even scarier, women might find magazines geared to their tastes.

"Maybe your 'hobby' will pay off, but retiring at full professor in twenty years will mean a comfortable retirement."

Bill shrugged. "My parents still live in the house I grew up in--little two-bedroom bungalow with a recreation room downstairs, a bedroom built into the attic. They're happy as clams. Did a bit of travel when Dad first retired, but enjoy living as they always have. Active in their church, faithful Republicans, civic-minded residents of a town they like, they don't need any more money than what they get from Social Security and a modest annuity."

"So, you're pretty sure the same will work for you."

Bill shrugged again. And Oscar knew he'd lost the battle.

He thought about the house his own father had built in retirement. And he meant "built," as the Swedish craftsman laid the foundation, put up the frame, installed plumbing and wiring, finished it inside and out. It was a simple shotgun house: living room, dining room, kitchen to the right; hall down the middle; bedroom, bath, bedroom to the left. He'd never wanted more.

Of course, Oscar's mother had. Growing up on a farm with three brothers, she'd dreamed of rising to a spacious brick home on a quiet city street. The Depression defeated that dream, and she'd settled for living close to her successful son (an hour away) and closer to her remaining brothers in Jefferson City. Still, they had enough money for their basic needs.

So, who would be the next head of the department? According to what Mid told him that night, it might well be Arthur James.

If she didn't stop by at some point in the evening these days, she did call and check on him. And tonight he learned over the phone more than he wanted to know — about campus politics and about the life of a divorcée.

"Ellie ran into Arthur today. Well, 'ran into' isn't the right word; he grabbed her."

"What? Where?"

"At Old and New Fashioned." This was a family-run clothing store on Main Street. "She was looking at herself in one of those three-panel mirrors, seeing what she thought of a new dress. He came up behind

276

her, put his arms around her waist, and said she looked good enough to take dancing."

"I guess he feels divorcees are vulnerable, especially pretty ones. Did she slap him?"

"She should have, but she was so shocked. She saw his face pop up right beside hers, and he was whispering in her ear with an unpleasant grin."

"Were you with her?"

"I was—on the other side of a rack of dresses. I heard her—not cry out exactly but say something louder than normal. So I came around to see what had happened."

"And you caught Arthur the magician in the act of casting a spell."

"He was certainly trying to. She told me later he had asked her to go to dinner with him. She declined, of course. Then he claimed she would sing a different tune when he was the new chair of the Physics Department. 'I'll be invited to fine dinners with deans, vice-presidents, and the Chancellor. A beautiful woman like you on my arm—' The man is coarse."

Oscar frowned. "Not an ideal dinner partner, to be sure. He'd be looking around the table at cleavages or under the table for legs, to see if there's a lady with better—features—he can pursue."

"It's something Elle and I have discussed—not having, you know, a man with us all the time."

"Well, if you need an escort, I can probably still serve in that capacity. If you let me."

Instead of the response Oscar was hoping for, the phone was silent. Then Mid said, "If all I needed was an escort, my life would be just fine right now. Unfortunately, a modern woman like me has greater desires. Good night, Oscar."

# Chapter Thirty-eight: Rehearsals

Oscar didn't understand it, but the final rehearsals for *Come Back, Little Sheba* were going well. Perhaps the quick design and building of a set had encouraged everyone to see their roles within a more concrete frame. It was simple--the cramped interior of a small middle-class home--but the set helped the actors find their places in many scenes. Oscar saw immediately that it fit the mood of the play--little color, no light from the outside, dingy and worn like the couple's marriage.

Ellie explained, "We tried to present a sense of dead ends, only a few windows, narrow doors, little room to maneuver around the furniture. The kitchen itself has Doc sitting only a few feet from Lola as she cooks or washes dishes. It's a table for two, but not romantic."

Just the kitchen and living room were represented on the stage, open to the audience with a wall between them. There was a door to the room Marie rented and another to the hall leading to Lola and Doc's bedroom. A tiny window, blacked over, was above the kitchen sink. The door to the outside was in a frame facing the audience.

"All that made construction easy," said Mid. "We used big sections and simple designs, mostly black and white. Well, you will see it a bit more clearly when we finish painting."

"I like it," Oscar said. "I'm not sure I had imagined anything except what was in the movie version; but the stage is always automatically more restrictive. The way you've made it open to the spectators should encourage them to feel they're in there with Lola and Doc."

Mid agreed. "The ones who escape, of course, are the kids, Marie, Bruce, and Turk. But we don't get to see where they go, their freedom."

"And that," sighed Oscar, "is more a fantasy than a reality."

Despite the gloomy subject of the play, coming early and staying late had been therapeutic for Oscar. It took his mind off his worries and provided unexpected pleasure. Ever since he got into the advanced study for his Ph.D., and then as a faculty member, he worked more and more alone. He had occasional students like Roger who met with him one-on-one. And a few genuine friendships resulted. But getting together regularly with a group was unusual for him.

Here he saw himself as a fellow thespian as well as director, often taking an actor's place for a scene, suggesting how he wanted the gestures, dialogue, poses. And if someone was late or had to miss a rehearsal, he took the role temporarily. He recalled many of the radio productions he'd written, sometimes later becoming the voice of one of the characters. Performance even in rehearsal was invigorating.

When the first complete run-through went longer than he thought appropriate, he began making small cuts to longer speeches. In a few cases, he rewrote lines. He hardly thought of himself as an author, but he was editing the script for this one production. His goal was to emphasize the key moments, allow them to be played out slowly and completely. Lola's state after Doc attacked her in a drunken rage is, he felt, a critical scene.

"Lola has been reliving her youth through Marie," he told Melissa Remington. "But now she's made to face the fact that she's not a young beauty fought for by different beaus. She's a dowdy middle-aged woman with a husband who's a drunk."

"I'm 'dowdy'?" laughed Melissa. Oscar knew full well that she was quite attractive. Not yet middle-aged. And lively.

"No, no, Lola is. And all she has is Doc, alcoholic chiropractor who dreamed of being a doctor. Her father won't even let her come home to visit because he's still angry that she got pregnant before she was married. After that she couldn't conceive a child, so she's realizing she must cling to what little remains in her life."

"Do I weep, then, or just tear up when I'm on the phone with my mom? Should I slump in my clothes, sag down to the floor, the cord almost around my neck?"

The phone was on a small shelf set into the living room wall close to the front door, as it had been in the Lindbloom home on the other side of town. Oscar thought how Mid, standing up, would talk with her mother back in New Jersey on her birthday and at Christmas. Neither used long distance much, for financial reasons; but he knew she missed her family on those occasions.

Oscar said to Lola, "You don't have a bounce in your step, to be sure. But how you say your lines will be as important as posture. The words have to be torn out of you. Each one is a confession of past failures, a desperate effort to build up something new, however small that might be."

"What do you suppose Doc is thinking?" said a voice behind Oscar. Turning, he found it was Ellie, who had been listening in the faux kitchen on the other side of the set wall. She had a paintbrush in one hand, and Oscar realized he'd forgotten she and Mid were putting in some finishing touches.

"Doc? You know, we don't see him since he went into a rage and was taken away. He's sleeping it off until morning."

"I understand that. Still, I was wondering if he's been having regrets. Or is it only when he returns and finds Lola has not left that he begins to reconsider his own actions."

"The way I see it," Oscar said, "he's still blaming Lola for everything. She seduced him, and he had to quit medical school to support her. Doc's kind of a lost

282

cause. The play's really more about Lola and her lost dreams."

"And Little Sheba is the dream," said Melissa. "The dog that ran off."

"Right. Always referred to but never seen, almost as if it never existed."

Bill Marks/Doc spoke up. "That's true for all of us, isn't it? We believe we possess certain memories, dreams, but we've made up most of them. We can't afford to look too hard for the 'girl I left behind' or 'the great job I should have had.' They're not real parts of our past."

"Speak for yourself!" said Melissa with a laugh. "I could have been a star."

Jan, who played Marie, added, "And I'm going to a be famous scientist and come up with a cure for some disease."

"Okay, okay, people. Let's see what we can do with this scene. It's all Melissa, but we can watch and offer advice."

Except for Mid and Ellie in the make-believe kitchen, they stepped down from the stage and took seats. The lights were on Lola.

Oscar tried to focus on Melissa's performance, but found himself studying the set. The basic structure had been in place for about two weeks, and it felt familiar. But now with more details finished it seemed even more familiar.

He glanced over at Mid painting a pretend oven under the fake stove. She was on the floor, her knees folded beneath her. She had put a smock on over her blouse and an old pair of slacks, both spattered here and there with dabs of paint. He admired her attention to detail, drawing not just knobs but the words "low," "medium," "high" around them.

When they had signed the contract for the new house, Oscar insisted that all finishing work be done by the builders. Mid had practically repainted the entire house on Limestone when they'd moved in, and he didn't want her to have to do all that a second time.

Most of the rooms in the other house had been a dingy white, and she wanted bright greens and blues. She knew that Oscar was busy with several new courses and a major research project, so she insisted on doing everything herself. The children were young and needed her attention, but she could work while everyone was at school.

She also sewed her own drapes, found old lamps in junk shops that could be fixed up, made slip covers for their aging living room furniture. A cherry breakfront carried back from New Jersey was refinished, and new coats of paint went on the children's furniture. She said she loved the challenge, and Oscar always remembered to say he was pleased with the results. In point of fact, those things didn't matter much to him.

Now Oscar realized her clock repair business was not just a new interest but a continuation of her desire to repair, improve, polish. The inner mechanisms interested her the most, but cleaning the cases and restoring the original finish also gave her great pleasure. Oscar could tell she was imagining each clock as if she'd purchased it as possible decoration for one room or the other.

To himself he concluded this was another good reason not to be building a lake house. She'd turn herself into a full-time construction worker. She deserved to do what she wanted now. They had the money and the time at last.

"Oh, hell," he thought, almost saying it out loud. *"This set is the first place we lived in, the second floor of the little house in Jeff City! She's recreated it exactly."*

# Chapter Thirty-nine: Costs

Harold Miller came to Oscar's office to give him what he termed good news and bad news. "Which would you like first?" he asked.

"Let's get the bad news over with." Oscar was trying to finish a set of quizzes from his quantum mechanics class before he raced off to do errands, eat, and get to the auditorium.

"It appears the dean is asking Arthur James to be department chair. The faculty is split, with no one member enjoying widespread support. And Arthur's fund-raising ability apparently trumps his, um, potentially embarrassing extracurricular activities."

"Money rules once again, the way of the future. I suppose there's nothing we can do but try to keep a close eye on him?"

Harold agreed. "Afraid so. But I can tell you from experience that a department head has only so much power. If the faculty gets angry, the dean will listen. And if he doesn't do the job the administration wants, he'll be out."

"It's the long-term direction of the department I worry about. More money for applied work, less for theoretical. More for lab equipment, not good teaching. You had a great vision when you took over, but I fear we'll be after short-term benefits now." He started to reach for his stack of quizzes, but then remembered: "Ah, I'm ready for the good news."

"I'm pretty sure it's good, but you'll need to confirm it." Harold handed him an envelope from the journal *Physics Theory*. Oscar knew what it meant.

He slipped his letter opener under the flap, sliced open the envelope, and read: "Congratulations. Your paper has been approved by our peer reviewers." It was the article he and Roger Stone had put together last spring from his preliminary work on his dissertation.

"You see? Your future is bright no matter who is chair of this department. And it means your student, Mr. Stone, is going to be getting a lot of attention when he applies for positions next year. I suspect he'll be able to write his own ticket. Good theorists are hard to find."

Oscar folded the letter back into the envelope and rose. "I'll call Roger and get him to drop by. This is good news indeed."

Having his work accepted for publication always pleased Oscar. And right now it confirmed his standing in the profession as an established researcher. But at the same time, it was not a step in a new direction. He was beginning to fear that all his hard work of the last twenty years was not leading to the personal satisfaction he had anticipated.

He and his colleagues around the country were keeping pace with the scientists of the Soviet Union in

The Cold War's battle of deterrence. But if all we accomplished was to stop Armageddon, was that enough of a positive outcome?

Oscar could not restrict the use others put to his discoveries. If it turned out his career had been devoted to providing a theoretical framework for the engineers of nuclear destruction, what good had he accomplished? If his grandchildren asked what he'd done in the (Cold) war, could he only say he had worked out sophisticated mathematical formulas about the properties of matter?

Taking up his briefcase, he prepared to leave. He hadn't been able to reach Roger by phone and decided he would put off congratulations for a day. That would give something to look forward to. He might need it if tonight's rehearsal went badly.

Picking up cleaning fluid for his contact lens on the way home, Oscar was delayed by the retired clock expert he met in line for the cash register. Mr. Agee told him, "Your wife has a gift."

"She has many gifts, but I assume you're referring to her ability to repair clocks."

"I am. It's not easy to diagnose problems with these older mechanisms. There was an explosion of American clock making early in this century with lots of companies producing different models every year. So, there's no authoritative manual for most of them."

"Ah, I understand. You have to study each one as an individual. But so far she's gotten them working, even if some have presented more challenges than others."

Oscar wanted to get away, stop by the house, make quick work of a TV dinner (chicken pot pie), and hurry to the auditorium for *Come Back, Little Sheba*'s final dress rehearsal. Some signs had been good lately--Melissa had become her part; but others were not--Mark kept wanting to be the center of things. Mr. Agee, however, wouldn't let him leave. "I can see that she enjoys the challenge. Still, to tell the truth, my friend, I'm a bit worried about her."

"How so?" They had both left the checkout and were standing on the sidewalk.

"I can't really say, but when she stopped by my house the other day, she was quite distracted. I don't mean to pry, of course, but she said you'd been so busy lately that she had more things to do than she could get to. Your children are pretty much out on their own, right? So maybe there are problems with the new house?"

"The house is fine, our children are fine. Listen, I appreciate your concern. And—and I'll make a point of having a talk with her about—everything, but I'm in a hurry right now."

"I understand. Again, I apologize for butting in, but she's such a sweet person." He squeezed Oscar's arm. "You're a lucky man, I'm sure you know that."

"I do, I do. Well, you take care of yourself, Mr. Agee. And enjoy your retirement years." Turning toward the door, he winced. Mr. Agee's wife had passed away a few years ago, and Mid had told him he was lonely without her. He had to do better about remembering such things.

Hurrying home, he thought, could Mid be going public with their situation? He was pretty sure she had agreed to keep it between them for now, but there could be rumors. Helping Ellie was good cover, but people might begin to rewrite the history of the past month.

As he entered the front door, the phone rang--his son Curtis. Oscar could tell that he really wanted to speak with his mom; but, after the perfunctory greetings and queries were over and she'd hadn't come on the line, he seemed to conclude that he'd better go ahead with his important news.

"So listen, Dad," he said. "I've got this great chance to do my fall semester in Israel. You know, live and study in the Holy Land, probably get to take some side trips to other countries like Egypt or Turkey."

Oscar was getting numb from surprises, so he just asked, "How much is it going to cost?" Given the fact that his son had said he couldn't talk very long tonight (his stack of quarters for the pay phone wasn't high), Oscar thought it an appropriate question.

"No more than if I were here. You see, you pay Westminster the tuition and room and board as usual, but the money goes to the university in Tel Aviv. And over the summer, I'll save a lot from my pay at the Survey for spending money over there."

"Isn't there travel? Perhaps you'll need extra equipment. It *is* the other side of the world."

Curtis seemed not to have thought of that. "Oh, yeah. I guess there would be airfare, but it's the opportunity of a lifetime."

Oscar sighed. "You do know there's a lot of violence in that country. They're almost at war with all their neighbors."

"Israel can take care of itself, Dad. They have the best military in the region."

"Well, your mother's out right now, but we'll talk about it." After a pause he added, "There's not a girl involved in this, is there?"

"Oops, my time is running out. So thanks, Dad. Yeah, see what Mom says. She's always been keen on the idea of travel. It's broadening, you know." The line went dead.

Turning the oven on and putting in his potpie, Oscar recalled how he'd wanted to travel at Curtis' age. But there had been no money; he had to support himself immediately after graduation. In fact, he had been working at part-time jobs since he entered high school. And he'd taken two years off from school to work full-time while his father recovered from an accident.

Mid came from more comfortable circumstances, but she too had felt an obligation to seek employment in the difficult years of the Depression. She saw her time with the Red Cross as a financial help to her family and as well as a service to the nation.

Oscar wondered if studying abroad would change Curtis' status with Selective Service. His sons were safe from the draft so long as they were in school. Having chosen to work in a civilian capacity during WW II himself, Oscar felt his children would help society more using their brains than carrying arms. (How his daughter went so far afield he still didn't understand!) But the war in Vietnam was heating up, so who knew what might happen in the future?

Now he needed to talk with Mid for all sorts of reasons; but he wouldn't be able to at tonight's rehearsal. She had volunteered to serve behind the scenes as a prompter. Ellie came also to handle any problems that might turn up with the set. But rehearsal and review would go late, and the two women would probably leave together before he was done with the cast.

Oscar knew the old adage: terrible dress rehearsal means great performance. When everything went better than he could have hoped, he sensed disaster ahead.

# Chapter Forty:
# Performances

"*Why*," thought Oscar to himself, "*did I for so many years take our only car to the campus every day and leave Mid at home with no transportation? It was only a mile, for heaven's sake! I could have walked or had her drop me off and take the car back home.*"

A voice inside answered: "*It was the nature of the times. Men, husbands, fathers were the breadwinners. They went out into the hard, cruel world every day to provide for their family. And the car represented both their ability and their commitment to do so. Mid was not being left at home; she was privileged to stay in a nice house in a good neighborhood surrounded by friends she could visit with over the back fence or on the sidewalk in front of her house.*"

Oscar was sitting with the Rockers of Age, hoping he could push such concerns as these to the back of his mind, enjoy the play, lose himself in the music. He'd had his final pep talk with the cast, the stagehands, the technicians. (Oh, yes--and the prompter.) Everyone was nervous but excited.

There was no orchestra pit in the auditorium, but the combo--piano, drums, bass, sax--had set up on the floor just to the side of the stage. They were about to play now before the curtain fell and as the audience filed in. They would start up again during the intermission and play briefly during the scene changes ("change music," Oscar said). Whenever he wasn't playing, Oscar followed the action on stage. But every once in a while, his mind went on its own way.

*"Yes, but when you first met Mid, she owned a car and you didn't. She'd been out on her own in the 'cruel, hard world,' as you call it, earning a living for half a dozen years. She'd even gone overseas to become a Donut Dolly, driving a Clubmobile, which, if necessary, she could repair on the side of the road."*

*"True, but that was during the war, when women were asked to work in factories, helping out on the home front while men went into battle. When peace came, we returned to the known and familiar. And it was good for everyone. The nation prospered, business expanded, we became one of the world's two super powers."*

On stage Marie was flirting with her two young admirers, Turk and Bruce. Lola vicariously enjoyed the situation. She also felt that, childless herself, she was acting as a mother to Marie. Doc, in the background, was a smoking powder keg, believing that he lost a promising medical career to Lola's seductive charms.

*"You made all the household rules from day one, didn't you: 'Come in or go out; go in or come out.' Mid never challenged you--at least in front of the children. You were king of your castle. But now your children are on their own and don't need to be safely housed in the home their parents provided. Mid is young and healthy enough to pursue any employment opportunity she finds, a trained medical technologist and/or aspiring clock repairman. Sitting at*

294

*home waiting for you to return from a long day of work isn't likely to be fulfilling."*

*"Hey, are you forgetting the pressures I face on campus? A new department chair, potential curriculum changes, new young faculty who want to challenge the full professors for the position as top dog. And let me tell you, delving into the atom or reaching out to the far reaches of space is exhausting mental work. I sometimes feel my brain is imploding under the weight of theoretical models. How can I recuperate every day unless someone distracts me with everyday affairs."*

Most of the music played by the Rockers of Age was from the period in which *Come Back, Little Sheba* is set; but several of Oscar's original compositions were also included. Turk had a martial song, heavy percussion emphasizing a forced march. Lyric lines swept Marie down a road of fantasy from present to past to future. Doc's glowering was accompanied by minor chords and uneven rhythms.

*"Hmm. Mid's job is to distract you?"*

*"You know what I mean."*

*"I fear that I do."*

*"Don't forget that she had help. The kids always wanted my attention when I got home. The boys and I would play catch. Carol would tell me about proofs she had discovered. I was pretty involved in all their games. Mid had time to knit and read."*

*"How involved were you in the children's schools? Did you go to PTA meetings, see that they had permission slips, bag lunches, the right clothes for the season? Isn't it true you just assumed all those things would be taken care of?"*

*"Yes, most of the time I did. But there are other things that generate a child's happiness: security and a conviction that your parents are taking care of you. We could pay for winter coats and bicycles, those summer trips to New Jersey. They knew where that money came from. They also knew I never, not once, had any interest in—any woman besides their mother."*

From time to time Oscar could see Mid behind the curtain with a script in her hands, moving to be close to the actors in case she needed to whisper a clue. Right now she was looking out at the audience and smiling. It was a broad smile. She glanced at Oscar, back at the seats, over to him. She nodded.

*"You know, we always celebrated her birthday. I insisted the kids make her a cake. I told them she had to have gifts under the Christmas tree just as they did."*

*"You gave her the same card every year on your anniversary, didn't you? She gave it back to you the next day, and you put it in your dresser door until the following year."*

*"She didn't want silly things--candy, flowers, expensive dinners out. She preferred to shop for her own jewelry. And I would go along to approve her choices."*

It was time for "Lover's Lament," Doc's melancholy catalog of his losses. Even as he launched into a long, slow solo, improvising with the soft snare behind him and the bass's punctuation, Oscar's mind wandered though a series of thoughts. Yes, he did enjoy unwavering support from Mid when he went to graduate school and then through all his years of teaching. It was not just that he came home to a hot

296

meal, clean sheets, the leisure to unwind. He also was praised, appreciated, respected.

How much better he's had it professionally than Doc. Oscar had earned the highest degree possible in his field; he had a steady, decent salary; there was remarkable stability to his position. Lola's husband had to drop out of medical school and become a chiropractor, sad fall. The cramped house and worn furnishings on the stage meant a struggle to achieve financial security.

But that still mattered less than the fact that he felt his wife did not love him. A wife who could not bear children. Marie was not a real daughter, and Lola's parents had separated themselves from her. She and Doc were alone together. Even the hope that, after the play's end, they would draw closer was faint.

*"I've been fortunate,"* Oscar concluded, *"working within a system in which I found the right place. But that system is changing, and now I have to change, too. I could pull back a bit from the relentless battle to be the best at whatever I do. Take more time to let Mid be good at what she does--as clock-maker or technologist or home decorator."*

*"I could take some vacations with my children (and one day grandchildren), not slip off to my study at every opportunity. And do I really need to teach summer school? We're financially stable, only Curtis, really, (and his crazy idea to take on causes) to worry about. So, a bit of travel for myself, as Mid has always wanted. At the very least, going to New Jersey more often."*

*"Can I take on a second home at Avalon Lake Estates? That may be too much. But perhaps I can join my literary*

*efforts with Mid's clock repair efforts, do some publicity for her--flyers, catalogs, advertisements. There might even be a book about clocks, the owners of different models from grandfather to cuckoo. Where did Charlotte get her clock, Little Ben, by the way? There's probably a story there. I would be working with Mid."*

Oscar finished his solo, and the piano smoothly picked up the melody. They would work back to the central motif and end together following the piano player's lead. He looked up again at the stage. Mid had the same strong smile. She nodded toward the audience. Was he supposed to notice something?

He looked at the crowd sitting in semi-darkness. There had a been a good turn-out, thanks in part to positive early reviews by both the university and the town paper. Not a full house, but close. And there would be another performance tomorrow night.

He was unhooking the neck cord from his saxophone so he could set it on its stand when he almost dropped it. There in the middle, halfway back, were all three of his children. Louis with Suzanne, who, seeing him look, gave Oscar a tiny wave. Curtis and a dark-haired, beautiful girl, Mediterranean complexion. And even Carol, his daughter, in uniform. How in the world!

He looked back to Mid, who was beaming. She put a hand on her heart and mouthed words he could read on her lips: "*I love you.*"

# Epilogue: Views

I told Curtis one day recently, "When rearview mirrors were made a federal requirement, I thought your father would launch into a tirade. After all, it was another government effort to say what individual citizens could do; and he was a pretty fierce individualist."

"He passed that tradition on to his children."

We were enjoying the lunch he'd brought with him to my little one bedroom apartment at the retirement home. It was the first warm day of spring, and I proposed we eat out on the patio.

"Don't forget, too, that I'm one of those stoic New Englanders, descended from Quakers who left England because of state-imposed religion. But Oscar endorsed the idea immediately."

"He might have asserted one of his favorite principles: most people are stupid. Therefore, in some cases they do need to be told what to do."

"He knew American car buyers would choose tinsel over safety devices. And, while he never talked much about it, the accident we had in Pennsylvania had a major impact on him."

Driving east one summer to see my mother, my sisters and brothers, we were hit from behind and driven into a low retaining wall around the parking lot.

"Ah," said Curtis, "so rearview mirrors were like seat belts for him."

Oscar was probably the first man in Fairfield to have a set of seat belts installed in his automobile. Cars were important to him, of course. And, if we weren't taking many long trips at that time, there were frequent Sunday drives out on Route 66, still his favorite highway (though it is now replaced by an interstate).

"Seat belts became mandatory about the same time that rearview mirrors did. And your dad realized that seat belts would have saved me a lot of pain and him his front teeth."

Curtis inspected his sandwich. "You know I remember very little about that event."

"Yes. The three of you weren't hurt because of the Nash's famous 'Bed in a Car.' You could raise the rear seat backs and hook them above the doorframes, creating a flat space below that extended into the front of the trunk. We padded that area so you children could lie prone, legs in the trunk, heads and shoulders on the rear seat cushions."

"Dad must have loved that Ambassador because he was always praising the design. I'm not sure I connected it to the fact that it kept us safe. About all I remember from that night is that some man helped me urinate by the side of the road."

"I'm not sure I knew about that; but, of course, I wouldn't have let you talk about such matters until you were at least sixteen! What else do you remember? You know my goal is to set the record straight here, to tell all--well, nearly all--of your family history. So I need to consider how some events were perceived by others."

"I have a clear view of a grassy ditch. A man is holding my hand, telling me it's all right to—'relieve myself'' there."

"Louis has a sharper image. He was riding in some kind of vehicle, sitting on a bench seat. In front were two beds with people lying on them. One person had blood all over his face."

"You or Dad? In an ambulance?"

"Yes. Dad had slammed into the steering wheel. I was thrown into the dash, both legs broken. You know that I still have metal pins. When the cold weather comes, they will ache. That's why I love days like today." I smiled up at the sun. "Let me get the cookies I baked."

When I returned, I said, "In those days we didn't linger over trauma. We felt it was best to move on, keep ourselves going as we had during hard times and the War. We didn't have--what do they call them?--'grief counselors'? And we didn't tell our children of our troubles."

"Right. Your generation was tough; we young people don't believe another of Dad's favorite adages: 'what doesn't kill you makes you stronger.'"

"And your children even less so. Do you know what happened after the accident?"

"Uncle John came to get us, didn't he? That may be something I heard you say later, not what I remember. I recall a night or two in a hospital, I think."

"Right. That was in Pennsylvania, close to the accident. You kept climbing out of the crib they had to put you in because they were out of beds."

"Hey, Louis had a bed; I deserved the same thing. Carol, now, she was a baby."

"And a girl," I huffed. "You boys always thought she had to be protected. And off she went to war. Turns out she was made of steel."

"She did better than I did!" Curtis agreed, though that wasn't true either. Both of my Vietnam vets served honorably. "But then we stayed at Uncle Axel's for — how long was it?"

"It was almost a month. I had to be able to walk with crutches. It was summer, though, so we didn't have to be back. We just lost our vacation that year."

Curtis laughed, "Louis and I didn't. We got to play with cousins and neighborhood kids. I remember having a lot of fun. And I even learned that boys and girls aren't exactly the same — in some physical characteristics."

"Your father insisted to me that he explained all that to you."

"Oh, he did. Drew some explicit drawings of— that area. But it's different in the flesh."

I smiled as he almost blushed. "So, you saw a woman's body, as you say, in the flesh? Perhaps *you'd* better clear the record here."

"It was a neighborhood girl. I don't even know how it happened exactly. We were all playing something--probably hide and seek--and she suddenly offered to let us see if we'd let her see. She might even have called it 'hide and peek.'"

"And you were willing?"

"Heavens, no! I was still a shy, small-town Midwestern boy. Now, Louis—"

"Humph. Obviously you didn't close your eyes when someone dropped his pants and she lifted her skirt."

"Mother! Your language. But, yes, it was a revelation etched in my mind forever."

"Well, it's good for me to know this. And, you see, it fits with the issue of rearview mirrors: sometimes to see where you're going, looking back is as important as looking ahead."

"Kind of contradicts another of Dad's favorite sayings, though," Curtis pointed out. "He liked to quote Satchel Paige--'Don't look back, something might be gaining on you.'"

I knew it was his MacBook, but I liked to feign ignorance some times. "Prepare to take notes."

As he obliged, I felt a satisfaction that I'd brought Oscar's and my story to a turning point. After he withdrew from consideration for the position at Enchantment College, we understood our future. We were stuck in a bigger house than we needed, like many Americans; and we had moved across town mostly because everyone else was doing the same thing.

But we'd come to realize that we--and the nation--needed to reshape our vision of ourselves and the world. It wouldn't be easy, but he and I knew we'd do it together. If what I've written about a dark time in my own life has the benefit of hindsight, I hope the lessons I learned forty years ago can help point others to a brighter future.

A new World Trade Center is going up in New York, and we seem to be closing out some far-off wars we thought would never end. The country is being reshaped by the Internet as the Interstate highway system reconfigured us many years ago. What a new American Dream will look like for my great grandchildren is something that I hope to see when I turn one hundred.

Ω

## Route 66 books by Michael Lund

**Growing Up on Route 66** — Michael Lund (2000) ISBN 1-888725-31-1 Novel evoking fond memories of what it was like to grow up alongside "America's Highway" in 20th Century Missouri. (Trade paperback) 5x8  260 pp

**Route 66 Kids** — Michael Lund (2002) ISBN 1-888725-70-2 Sequel to *Growing Up on Route 66*, continuing memories of what it was like to grow up alongside "America's Highway" in 20th Century Missouri. (Trade paperback) 5x8 270 pp,

**A Left-hander on Route 66**--Michael Lund (2003) ISBN 1-888725-88-5. Twenty years after the fact, left-hander Hugh No one appeals a wrongful conviction that detoured him from "America's Main Street" and put him in jail. But revealing the details of the past and effecting a resolution of his case mean a dramatic rearrangement of his world, including troubled relationships with three women: Linda Roy, Patty Simpson, and Karen Murphy. (Trade paperback) 5x8 270 pp

**Route 66 Spring**-- Michael Lund (2004) ISBN: 1-888725-98-2. The lives of four young Missourians are changed when a bottle comes to the surface of one of the state's many natural springs. Inside is a letter written by a girl a dozen years after the end of the Civil War. Lucy Rivers Johns ' epistle contains a sad story of family failure and a powerful plea for help. This message from the last century crystallizes the individual frustrations of Janet Masters, Freddy Sills, Louis Clark, and Roberta Green, another group of Route 66 kids. Their response to the past charts a bold path into the future, a path inspired by the Mother Road itself. (Trade paperback) 5x8 270 pp.

**Miss Route 66**--Michael Lund (2004) ISBN 1-888725-96-6. In the fourth novel of Michael Lund's Route 66 Novel Series, Susan Bell tells the story of her candidacy in Fairfield, Missouri's annual beauty contest. Now married and with teenage children in St. Louis, she recounts her youthful adventure in this small town along "America's Highway." At the same time, she plans a return to Fairfield in order to right injustices she feels were done to some young contestants in the Miss Route 66 Pageant. (Trade paperback) 5 X8, 260 pp, **Audio book** on 5 CD's ISBN 1-888725-12-5

**Route 66 to Vietnam** Michael Lund (2004) ISBN 1-59630-000-0 This novel takes characters from earlier works in the Route 66 Novel Series farther west than Los Angeles, official destination of the famous highway, Route 66. Mark Landon and Billy Rhodes find the values they grew up on challenged by America's role in Southeast Asia. But elements of their upbringing represented by the Mother Road also sustain them in ways they could never have anticipated. . (Trade paperback) 5 X8, 270 pp,.

**Audio Book on CD — Route 66 to Vietnam** ISBN: 1-59630-011-6 Michael Lund's fictional commentary from the viewpoint of a draftee. by Michael Lund unabridged 6 CD's --9 hours running time

**Route 66 Chapel** Michael Lund (2006) ISBN 1-59630-012-4 Route 66 Chapel, Michael Lund (2006) (Trade paperback) 5 X8, 260 pp. When the forces of progress threaten the foundation of small-town life — a small church — five senior citizens, a mysterious newcomer, and one young couple band together in an unlikely campaign to save it. The embattled meeting point of old and new is Route 66 Chapel, a building curiously linked to America's "Mother Road."

**Route 66 Choir-- A Comedy (2010) Michael Lund** ISBN 9781596300583 284 pp 5" x 8" In Route 66 Choir Stanley

308

Measure takes early retirement just before September 11, 2001, and his impulsive decisions participate in an unraveling of confidence in the American way of life. His wife Felicia finds that everything she holds dear is in danger of coming apart: her marriage, her church, her business, and even her country. Who or what can orchestrate the recovery of harmony necessary to sustain the spirit of the Mother Road?

**Route 66 Sweetheart** (2011) ISBN 9781596300705    304pp 5"x8". This first of a  novel series chronicles an American family during times of peace and war from 1915 to 2015. The first book, *Route 66 Sweetheart*, is set mostly in and around Rutherford, New Jersey, during the 1930s, where a young woman who traces her ancestry back to the early New World settlement of Nantucket comes to maturity during the Depression In the shadows of an emerging World War II.

**Route 66 Dreamer**  (2013)  ISBN 978-1596300835 318 pp 5"x8". Route 66 Dreamer  features the son of a Swedish immigrant who pursues his dreams of American success in Kansas and Missouri in the early 1940s. However, in both books some family members move away to distant countries and unexpected challenges.

# *Short Stories*

**How to NOT tell a War Story** (2010) ISBN 9781596300798 (2012) 298pp 5"X8", A collection of stories about veterans who, though they were in a war, have no traditional war stories to tell. As they move into retirement forty years after the experiences, they begin to wonder if somehow there isn't something more to say about how their service affected their lives. Among other things, they come to appreciate the lovers, friends and family who helped them shape a new, post-war identity.

Michael Lund's five-volume novel series chronicles an American family during times of peace and war from 1915 to 2015. The first book, *Route 66 Sweetheart* (2011), is set mostly in and around Rutherford, New Jersey, during the 1930s. *Route 66 Dreamer* (2012) features the son of a Swedish immigrant who pursues his dreams of American success in Kansas and Missouri in the early 1940s. However, in both books some family members move away to distant countries and unexpected challenges.

The third volume, *Route 66 Looking-glass* (2013), takes place primarily in Missouri in 1965, but characters also travel far from home and familiar experiences. Book Four (2014) follows another generation of family members, this time from Missouri to Southeast Asia where many learn, sadly, "how to not tell a war story." In the final volume of the series (2015), the next generation travels to Europe and the Middle East to understand their identity in a multi-national community.

He folded his napkin. "I never knew you and Dad had that rough time. You did as well to keep your temporary 'separation' from us as you kept quiet about the accident. When we went home for *Come Back, Little Sheba*, you were so happy for him and so proud of him. And he praised the set over and over, said it reminded him of fundamental things in his life."

"I don't ever think I believed we could be apart, but I had to do something to—to change the way we were living together. And, bless him, he figured it out by himself. When I told him that Ellie was doing all right on her own now, he knew that was my way of saying I couldn't be without him anymore than he without me."

"You've passed that conviction on to your children as well," Curtis admitted.

"That gives me more happiness than just about anything we ever did in life. But, you know, you all had your struggles, too. And that's where this story goes next. Oscar and I still figure in the history, but we'll be in the rearview mirror of the family saga."

"Yikes! You mean I have to spill the beans about all the bad things Louis did as a boy and how Carol isn't at all the superstar scientist you think she is?"

"I already have your letters. And Carol kept a diary when she was overseas, which I also have. Louis, of course, wrote in a journal as meticulously as you'd expect a lawyer to do. I suspect he'll let me see an edited version. So, you have your—device there—"